THE LONG WAY HOME

E. G. STONE

For Sammy

CONTENTS

1

———

HOMESICK

"Tilt your head to the left. Now, look at the camera—the *lens* this time—and try to act like you're enjoying yourself," I said. Agravane, sitting at a wooden table with books and pens and things stacked up beside him, a coffee mug with the logo for the brand I was supporting directly in front of him, looked at the camera and glared. It wasn't quite the image I was going for. I suffered so greatly for my marketing endeavours. "Take a sip of the coffee."

"I don't actually like coffee, Cal," Agravane complained. "Why do I have to do this? Why can't you?"

"You have to do it because you embody the immortal prettiness and grace that comes with the magical beings of Elsewhere, to whom we are trying to market this coffee. I can't do it because, for all my intelligence and skill in the marketing realm, and the fact that I can't die, I am still human. And humans are prey.

You don't buy drinks meant for prey." I gave a decided sniff and took a few more shots, fairly certain that none of them would work.

My name is Cal Thorpe, and despite being the premiere—also the only—marketing agent in all of Elsewhere, no one seemed to take me seriously. Not Yolanda, my assistant, not Agravane, my junior marketing agent, and certainly not Death, my boss. Okay, Death took me seriously, but that was just because he was a serious person. The same could not be said of my employees. Behind us, Yolanda was fervently trying to work, though her typing had gotten significantly louder in the time since we started arguing about the coffee. I think it was meant to stifle the giggles.

"And we can't hire models because...?" Agravane took a disdainful sniff of the coffee and plastered on a fake smile.

"We can't hire models because they won't understand what we're trying to do. That, and the last time I tried to get hired help to come to Death's lands for such a thing, I ended up having to pay emotional damages."

"Oh, come on, that was months ago. Death had a cold. It wasn't our fault he sneezed right as we were trying to take the picture."

"Just sit still and try to look like you can take on the world. Can you at least do that?" I adjusted the camera again, ready to snap a picture as soon Agravane actually cooperated.

He smirked. "I may not be able to take on the world, but I can certainly take on you."

I snapped the picture, capturing that arrogant snide posture. None of the people who would be seeing this on social media or wherever would know that the arrogance was to do with his beating me soundly in every self-defence session that we had participated in over the last six months. Agravane had been trying to teach me the fine art of fending off beings rather a lot stronger than me, and certainly more dangerous. Since I was just Cal Thorpe, human in a world of magic, it was turning out to be a rather unproductive task. That is, in the last six months, I had learned how to duck, how to run, how to wail in what Agravane would call terror but I would call strategic retreat, and land one punch. Yolanda had watched our sessions once and promptly declared that I was not a being made for self-defence, or fighting at all.

Thank goodness Death had hired me to do marketing, not be some ninja assassin or similar nonsense. Of course, such an attitude hadn't helped much in the last couple of years. I had investigated a murder, travelled through time, lost my soul, dealt with the Taxman, been killed multiple times, developed an irrational fondness for coffee, and was currently also contracted out as a gofer for Life. All these circumstances could have been vastly improved by my not being vastly unprepared for highly-powerful magical creatures.

However, since I was now also a Reaper, some sort of semi-sentient magical energy living inside me—I had named it Sebastian—Agravane insisted that we continue with the pointless effort of trying to teach me how to defend myself. I was of the opinion that, considering I couldn't die, despite numerous efforts from various parties in that regard, such efforts were unnecessary. Once I did regain use of my soul, and could therefore die in a permanent fashion, I assumed that it would be far safer for me to remain where I was; I had no qualms whatsoever about hiding. If I did have to venture out into the unknown of Elsewhere, then I would simply charm my way out of trouble.

It had worked for me in the past. Admittedly, not as well as I would like. It was a work in progress.

Of course, that plan was contingent on me actually finding my soul, and I was nowhere near that goal. Six months ago, Neja the djinn had stopped by after a job she had taken in the mortal realm, giving me a piece of paper from 700 years ago in Croatia. On it was written *the employment was a mistake*, and it was signed. By me. In my handwriting.

Every test that I had run on the document suggested that it was, in fact, real. Since I had never been to Croatia, either in the present or the distant past, I could only assume that my soul was the one who wrote it. Which was really annoying, because I thought I was better than leaving cryptic remarks behind. If I were going to leave myself a terribly old document, then I could at least do my best to make sure that it made sense.

Anyways.

I snapped another picture, though we had probably done all we could do for the day, and gave up. "Fine. Go do your marketing things. I think the dwarf clans wanted to work with you again, something about the upcoming coronation of their seventh princess being a rather important event."

"I thought we agreed to foist that off on Yolanda," Agravane said, though he did push back from the table with great speed. I rescued the undrunk cup of coffee and popped it into the microwave. It wasn't really as good when you reheated it, but considering it was still the best coffee I'd ever had, I wasn't going to complain. In exchange for marketing this particular brand, I got a lifetime supply, the result of a bargain made in the goblin market with a brownie while I was less than coherent. Still, it all worked out.

Mostly.

"And I told you that it wasn't Yolanda's fault you couldn't pronounce their names. All you had to do was spell them correctly and it would all be fine." No matter how badly Agravane spelled, the dwarf clans seemed to only want to work with him in their marketing endeavours. And, since I was the boss, I was happy to foist them off on somebody else.

Despite being Death's official marketing agent, my firm was doing quite well. My reach had spread throughout Elsewhere to the point where I was having to turn away clients who wanted my assistance in their marketing endeavours. Coming from the mortal realms, I never would have expected that anything magical would require such extensive marketing and public relations, but the denizens of Elsewhere were just as pleased to utilise my services as those back in London. As it distracted me from my Reaper duties, which I was still trying to avoid and had managed to ignore fairly successfully thus far, and kept me out of the way of both Life and Death—to whom I owed work —I was pleased.

Well, as pleased as you can be when you have no soul. My emotions were still muted, as though I was experiencing them behind a thick veil. When they weren't muted, I was either expounding on the wonders of coffee or wildly erratic. Yolanda and Agravane said that my grumpy attitude wasn't diminished in the slightest. Plus, having Sebastian writhing around inside me, exerting its influence when things were getting slightly dicey, was not so much helpful as throwing petrol on a brushfire.

Still, the last six months had been blissfully quiet.

It worried me.

"You have that look again," Yolanda said, finally looking up from her computer. Yolanda was my rock troll assistant, the cheerful presence in the office, and also very good at reminding me of normal things that I was meant to be doing. I've discovered that when you're without a soul, you don't actually feel all that much urgency to complete tasks, and more importantly, you forget the little things. Like social niceties. Or the purpose of straws.

"Specify which look," I said, taking a sip from my coffee.

"The one where you're thinking about why Life hasn't contacted you to do work for her, or why Death hasn't sent you on a job in a while. It's a rather specific look." Yolanda tapped her lips with a pen, then caught wind of my latest expression and quickly went back to work.

I had never thought myself the sort of person to worry when things were going well until I started working for Death. I think it rather just came in the job description. As it was, six months of quiet had been absolutely blissful and marvellous and nerve wracking. I didn't trust it one bit.

"Seriously," Agravane said, looking up from the massive Dwarven dictionary that he was thumbing through on his desk. "What's going on, Cal? You seem on edge."

"I told you," Yolanda said, frowning at Agravane, "he has the look where he worries about why Life hasn't contacted him and—"

"Enough," I grumbled, almost slamming my coffee mug on my desk. As that would likely spill some of the precious liquid, I held back, setting it on the desk with a clunk, but very little force. "Things are fine, okay? Let's just get on with doing the marketing tasks for the day. I want to edit those pictures for—"

The door burst open.

I should have known better than to announce that things were fine in a semi-loud voice. Pretty much like clockwork, whenever I did that Life or Death would swan through my door and demand that I perform some ridiculously difficult task. The last one had been petsitting for Death while he was on jury duty. I had nearly started a war between Faerie nations. And then I was attacked by Death's cat.

This time, it was Life striding through the door of my office as though she owned the place. Given her general arrogance, she acted like that almost all the time. Life was the sort of being that it was hard to look away from; while I couldn't tell you what colour her hair was, or what sort of figure she had, what colour her eyes were, or even her skin tone, I could tell you that she was the most stunning person I had ever met. Life was ever-changing and always beautiful, tempting, and overwhelming. This time, though, she was wearing a smile that told me she was absolutely up to no good.

"Hello, Cal!" Life said, moving towards me and just about wrapping me in a hug. I stepped back a very definitive step. It's always a bad thing when Life gets touchy feely. "Oh, piffle, is that any way to greet your employer?"

"Death is my employer. I just do things for you on occasion," I said, a very slight amount of alarm in my voice. That was more than I usually felt, so there was definitely something going on. "Are you here to have me do a job? I am rather busy—"

Life waved a dismissive hand. "No. It's no fun to have you do a job when you're *expecting* it, is it?"

"I told you that you had that look," Yolanda whispered, her voice carrying across the room. Life snapped her ever-changing eyes to my assistant. Yolanda sank into her chair and tried to look engrossed in whatever she was doing. Life quirked an eyebrow and gave my assistant the once-over that you usually got at a bar on a Friday night.

"I assume you're here for me," I said, tilting my head expectantly. Life's gaze lingered on Yolanda for a moment before sliding back to me. She smiled and put a hand on her hip.

"Of course, Cal. Why else would I bother coming all the way to my husband's lands? None of his creatures are all that interesting to me," she said, stepping forwards with a purr in her voice. I sighed overloudly and waited.

Life frowned, then sat back on my desk. "You're absolutely no fun, do you know that?"

"I am plenty of fun," I retorted, though I think the remark would have had more of an impact if I were not speaking in monotone. "Just ask..." I paused, trying to come up with a name that wasn't Yolanda or Agravane, or any of the people I had run into while Life was around. "Is there a reason why you're here?"

"I'm here because—"

The door slammed open again. This time, Death strolled through, looking impeccable and dangerous in a three piece black suit with a crimson tie, his hands stuffed into his pockets, his skin the colour of a black hole and his eyes nothing more than voids into the dark. He paused for a moment when he spotted Life, then heaved a sigh that was far more dramatic than my own.

"What are you doing here?" Death drawled. Life huffed and crossed her arms.

"I'm here for my own reasons. I don't need to have an excuse to talk with Cal, as he's contracted to me," Life sniped, reaching out to pat my arm as if I were some pet of hers. I sidestepped and leaned my weight on Yolanda's desk, deciding that it would be better if I didn't get between Death and Life.

Separate, they were dangerous and difficult. Together, they were the equivalent of a nuclear explosion, the aftermath of which was usually my responsibility to clear up.

"She said she wasn't here for a job," I reported to Death.

Death sighed again, this time a sound of long-suffering exasperation. "You're here about *that*? I told you that I would take care of it."

"Pah," Life snapped with a wave of her hand. "You would have just sent him on his merry way, with no extra explanations or assistance or any meddling at all. What fun is that?"

Death rolled his eyes, which was actually quite impressive since he doesn't have any eyes. "What extra explanations could possibly be required? What extra assistance? Cal has proven himself incredibly capable. He is a Reaper, wife, and can fend for himself. And no one needs your meddling."

"Boring," Life said, tossing her head. "Just because he's a Reaper doesn't mean he might not need some extra—"

"Will someone please explain to me what is going on and why I might need extra help?" I asked. "My coffee is getting cold, and I have to start editing these photographs for a social media campaign."

Life and Death looked at me, then looked at each other, exchanging identical sympathetic glances. The hair on the back of my neck started to stand on end. While I couldn't tie the feeling to any particular emotion, Sebastian did open an eye inside me and give a worried grumble.

I understood the thought exactly.

Death turned and closed the door behind him, as though anyone who might hear of the situation wasn't already in the room. I mean, really, I work with a rock troll and an aurai with social media access at their fingertips at any given time. What sort of secrets did he think were going to be kept by a closed door?

"Before I discuss the details, Cal, I am informing you that I am giving you two weeks' vacation to sort this out," Death said slowly. I blinked, a strange surge of emotion unfurling in my chest. I think, had I been able to really understand what it was, I would have fainted in sheer delight at being given vacation time. Finally! I had been wanting a vacation since I started, and I could think of several really nice beaches that I would be glad to visit. I would pack some shorts and t-shirts and a nice Panama hat and—

I narrowed my eyes suspiciously. "You're not giving me vacation time to go relax on a beach, are you?"

Death shook his head. "No, Cal."

I turned to glare at Life. "And if you're involved, then that means it's really big. Change a person's perspective and potentially cause a serious life change sort of big."

Life grinned at me. No shame whatsoever.

"Cal, I think you should go home for a bit." Death spoke these words with such genuine concern that I was absolutely certain he had just announced the world was ending. Or something similar.

"Why?" I asked, folding my arms. It wasn't that I didn't want to go back to London. I really liked London. But Death had removed me from the fate of the world when he first hired me, and going back home would likely involve being tied up in the fate of the world. Frankly, that sounded like a bad idea.

"It's your cousin," Death said, as if breaking terrible news to a child. "He's gotten himself into a bit of trouble..."

"Oh, just tell him already! Your cousin has managed to get involved in the trade of Dragonwort and is about to tip the balance of magic in the mortal realm in a way that hasn't been seen in *centuries*." Life clapped her hands gleefully and, if I didn't know better, looked like she was going to cackle her joy.

"Uh-huh," I said. I looked at the clock on my phone and noted that there were only a couple more hours in my work day. I decided that I was going to have pizza for dinner. Maybe open a bottle of wine. Watch a movie.

"You don't seem concerned," Death said gravely. He looked to Yolanda and Agravane. "Is this his soulless nature shining through?"

"Nope!" Yolanda said cheerfully. "That's more of an empty sort of expression, like the words just floated through his mind and went right out the other side. Right now, Cal just doesn't care."

Death frowned. Life gaped. I wondered whether the microwaved coffee was still warm, or if I would just have to make a whole new pot. I briefly considered tea, but decided that would be too much effort, when I already had the coffee grounds ready to brew.

"Regardless," Death said at last, "neither Life nor I can allow the balance of magic to tip in the mortal realms. Not in so dramatic a fashion. While there are those who are aware of Elsewhere and the true nature of things, letting the entire mortal realms know of our existence would be a really bad idea. You shall have to go home and deal with things."

I opened my mouth to argue, or ask questions, or anything, but it was too late. Life and Death both surged for me like predators after a really juicy piece of meat, intent plain in their eyes. They each touched me on the forehead and I barely had time to consider complaining before the world shattered into a million tiny pieces and I developed a headache that roared through me like a forest fire.

I appeared on a street outside a familiar row house

in the middle of London. Before I had time to register just how much pain I was in, something ran towards me and nearly tackled me, wrapping its arms around my middle and squeezing the air out of my lungs.

"Cal!" I recognised the voice and the person. My cousin looked up at me with an overly cheerful expression, eyes wide. "I thought you were dead!"

2

WELCOME HOME

*N*ow before I get into analysing *that* particular statement, I should tell you a little bit about my family. Unfortunately.

While I would be quite happy to claim that I sprang fully-formed from the brain of some sort of marketing master, the truth is that I belong to a long line of Thorpes, spelled with an 'e'. This is rather different from the Thorps spelled without an 'e', who are an entirely different family and have absolutely no relation. I know this because my great uncle Wilfred did some research, having grown tired of being mistaken for a Wilfred Thorp, no 'e', who happened to live in the same town and had several profitable patents to his name.

Moving on.

Generally speaking, the Thorpe family from which I come are a stodgy, traditional British family who are more than happy to trace their roots back through the days of various monarchs and wars. We were never a very large clan, and had a distinct inability to move anywhere besides England, though I did have an aunt who moved all the way to Stromness in Scotland. She never actually communicated with the family, though. As a whole, the Thorpe clan is fond of tea, making a decent living, staying far away from politics, and following every traditional English pastime with great reverence. This includes cricket, the occasional rugby, reading the Sunday paper, having tea at prescribed times of day and, very rarely, going to the pub to watch the football match.

There are two exceptions to this outline in my family.

Me, as I preferred coffee and climbed my way up the marketing ladder of a respected firm, which would hopefully jumpstart my career into a globally-renowned marketing name. Unfortunately, I got hired by Death long before this could happen, but it did mean that I moved far, far away from England.

Then, there is my cousin. Basil. Baz for short.

He has absolutely no liking for either coffee or tea, preferring energy drinks as his pick-me-up. His ambitions went as far as working with the local gangs at a car chop shop, and one very unfortunate summer on a roadtrip through America. He has a distinctly cheerful attitude and the ability to talk as loudly as any tourist. He also doesn't like football, cricket, or rugby, though he did develop a strange fondness for the Canadian hockey league.

That's only the beginning.

When Life and Death appeared in my office, telling me that my cousin had gotten into some trouble and was somehow involved with the magical future of the entire mortal realms, I had hoped—for a brief moment—that they were referring to anyone in my family other than Baz. I have two cousins on the other side of the family who work together at a small financial firm and have gotten into exactly no trouble ever, that I am aware.

I should have known better.

Baz was, in looks, completely unlike me. His mother was Turkish and his father was fair with vibrant red hair, so Baz had a sort of fascinating combination of golden skin and copper coloured hair, brown eyes and a grin that caused women who didn't know him to swoon. I, on the other hand, was average height, had average brown hair that barely curled, wore glasses, and much preferred a well-tailored suit to whatever get-up Baz was currently wearing.

Speaking of, I pushed him back and frowned. "Are you wearing plaid joggers? With a striped t-shirt?" I didn't think the Birkenstocks straight from California that he had on his feet were worth mentioning.

Baz grinned. "Yeah! It was all that was clean, but I think I like it."

"It's very...loud," I said with as much honesty as I could muster. Baz laughed, uproariously and with great vigour, and slung his arm around my shoulder.

"It's good to have you back, Cal! Where have you

been? I mean, everyone thought you died. Seriously, your mum held a funeral and everything." Baz pulled me along as he talked, dragging me up the steps to the unfortunately-familiar row house and practically kicking the door open. "Hey, Auntie Teresa! I have a surprise for you!"

"Since when were you living with my mum?" I asked, deciding that it would be better if I didn't discuss the whole dead-not-dead thing. It was a rather complicated story, after all. Not to mention, I wasn't actually certain how much I *could* tell people, given that Death had removed me from the fate of the world and all. Of course, I had been transported to just outside my mother's house, so perhaps I was being given carte blanche. Or perhaps this was one of those things that Death hadn't wanted to tell me.

Baz shrugged and leaned against the door to close it behind us, the frame having warped years ago. I had been going to fix it, before the whole Death thing. I added it to my mental to-do list for this situation. Figure out what Baz broke and fix it, replace the door frame.

"Auntie T gave me a place to stay after I had to leave my last place. Landlord sold the building and some big construction people came by to tear it down the next day. Whoosh! Boom! Gone. Apparently there was some sort of toxic thing in the building and it needed to be replaced," Baz said with a grin, illustrating the destruction of his building with his hands, as well as sound effects.

Like I said, my cousin and I were really not very much alike. He was great fun at parties, though.

I opened my mouth to say more when a shuffling sound caught my attention. Or, rather, a sort of delicate stepping that just happened to be taking place in house slippers. A moment later, and my mother appeared in the hallway, wearing the same embroidered house slippers that she'd worn for years, as well as a vintage designer dress, her hair in perfect waves on her head, and a face full of makeup that looked like it had been professionally done.

I got my preference for a well-turned out look from her. I've been told that there are a few other personality similarities, but I never saw it.

My mother put her hands on her hips and frowned at me. Then, she sighed and started back towards the kitchen, waving her hand almost dismissively. "Come on, then. I'll make us a pot of tea."

Baz clapped me on the arm so hard that it started tingling. "Isn't this great? It'll be just like old times!"

He scrambled down the hall after my mother while I rubbed the tingles out of my arm and tried now to scowl fiercely. Presumed dead for two plus years and this was the greeting I got. It was no wonder I didn't really look back after being hired by Death.

I strode after my cousin and my mother, wondering if it would be possible to have this whole situation cleared up by suppertime. Maybe I could take the rest of those two weeks and lounge on a beach in some tropical location. Somehow, I doubted it.

The kitchen was almost exactly as I remembered; the layout was the same, with a central island containing the stove and oven, a bright green kettle already whistling away. There was a small table in the corner by some bay windows, and Baz was already sitting before a plate of iced biscuits, eating merrily. Of course, the kitchen was also absolutely nothing like I remembered, with the counters being made of a dark green granite, the cabinets done in a lovely cherry wood, the walls painted a completely different colour, all new appliances and a glass vase on the table that was, if I knew my art, worth several hundred pounds.

"You did some redecorating, I see," I said, sitting next to Baz and watching my mother pour the boiling water into a pot, swirl it around, pour it out again and then begin the proper ritual of making tea. Her movements were practised, precise, completely calm.

Is it so wrong that I wanted perhaps just a little emotion at my sudden resurrection?

"I used your life insurance policy," my mother said calmly. "I was the beneficiary, after all."

Baz thumped his hand on the table and gave an enthusiastic nod. "Yeah, what was that about? I thought you would have left at least some to me!"

I pushed my glasses up my nose and did my best not to sniff. "I rather assumed that you would find a way to fund yourself before I died."

My mother poured the tea into cups and then put them on the table. She sank into a chair opposite me and took a graceful sip before setting her cup neatly into her saucer and fixing me with one of her signature Looks. It was the sort of look that I had practised and could never quite manage, the sort of look that told you things were about to become Very Bad and you were A Complete Idiot.

"So, should I expect an explanation as to why my son was declared dead, why I held a funeral and informed the entire family of my son's death, and then my son shows up at my doorstep without so much as a telephone call?" Her voice had gone very precise, and the repeated use of the phrase "my son" was a pretty good indication that I had well surpassed the Complete Idiot stage and moved into the Shall Never Be Spoken Of Again stage.

This was about as good as I was going to get as far as emotional reunions went.

"It wasn't my choice," I said, doing my best to put at least a small amount of apology into my tone. "The situation came upon me before I could make any sort of preparations or explanations. I was informed that I wouldn't ever be coming back, so you can imagine my surprise when I was, ah, sent here."

Maybe they would just accept my mysterious answer and assume that I had been kidnapped by the government, or some criminal enterprise, then move on. You know, the standard "if I don't talk about my problems then they don't exist" philosophy.

Granted, I was talking to the two people who would be least likely to ignore my subtle hint to not ask questions. My mother because she was stubborn, determined to know everything, and had a regular disdain for people who refused to provide appropriate answers. Baz because he just had no sense of propriety.

"Whoa! Did you get attacked? Kidnapped? You working for some sort of secret organisation so you can market their skills without actually letting the whole world know about them and then they traded your marketing ability for knowledge about how to kill people?" Baz's eyes got wider at every word, until I was fairly certain they would pop out of his skull. His theory was terrifyingly accurate, too, which worried me. I narrowed my eyes.

"Calvin Montgomery Thorpe, if you do not tell me the whole truth right this minute, I will turn you out on the street and never speak with you again." My mother narrowed her eyes far better than I did.

"You won't believe the truth," I said flatly. I would like to say that I was flat because my current soulless state was not letting me feel any emotions, but I fear that it had nothing to do with my lack of a soul and more to do with the fact that this was normal for my interactions with my family. I did my best to avoid strong emotions around them. It was far safer.

Of course, not having a soul did nothing to help the situation.

"Speak," my mother ordered. Baz sat up straighter, ready for the story.

I silently cursed Life and Death for putting me in this situation. Then, because one disobeyed my mother at their own peril, I told them the truth. Every bit of it.

I started with being hired by Death, then having to solve a murder he did not commit. I told them about going back in time to fix the relationship problems between Life and Death and meeting Machiavelli along the way. I told them about my missing soul. I told them about my arrangement with Al Capone's soul, and the resulting fiasco in modern day Chicago. I told them about acting as Death's proxy and my subsequent discovery of being a Reaper. I told them about preventing a war in Faerie while pet sitting, and the discovery of the note that was potentially left by my soul. I told them about Yolanda and Agravane, about Mercy and Justice, about Neja.

"...and here I am," I said, very definitively not telling them why, exactly, I had been sent home. I decided that it would be better to simply deal with Baz without my mother around. Why I was here to deal with a magical problem rather than simply visit my family. And also to spare Baz my mother's scrutiny when I told him it was his fault I was home. There were some things better left unsaid.

We had finished off the entire pot of tea during my tale, and Baz had eaten all the iced biscuits. Now, he was gaping at me like I'd just sprouted two heads. My mother sat back in her chair, her posture as straight as ever, and gave a dramatic sigh.

"You don't have a soul," she said, giving me what in anyone else I would have called a speculative glance.

I nodded.

"I suppose I won't make you go to church on Sunday, then," she sniffed. With that, she rose, picked up the tea pot and took it to the sink. Then, she started for the door to the kitchen. "I have some things to do. You may sleep in the guest room. There's some money in the desk drawer if you go out. Do try to call if you'll be out late."

Then, she left.

Baz continued to gape at me. "Dude!"

I sighed. "Yes?"

"You can't *die*?!" Baz looked like he wanted to poke me, see if I was real.

"Why is it, out of all the pieces of my story, you find that part the most difficult?" I asked, my tone flatter than it was before. I got the distinct impression that I was becoming annoyed. Had I been feeling things normally, I believed that I would be really very annoyed. Possibly annoyed enough to yell or shake my cousin until he started spouting sense. As it was, Sebastian just rolled over inside me and huffed deeply.

Baz shrugged. "Well, frankly, you're not creative enough to make the rest of it up."

I sighed again. "No, I cannot die."

"Cool," Baz said, grinning again. "So, I suppose I should take you around, since you've been gone for so long. You know, meet the friends, say hi to everyone, show you the things that have changed."

"I *am* here for a reason," I said. I wondered whether

I could get some coffee soon, if it would even out my irascibility. Probably not.

"Sure, sure, no worries. You know that place a few streets over, where they used to sell those pastries?" Baz pushed back from the table and scratched his stomach as if he hadn't just eaten a full plate of iced biscuits. "The owners sold it and some really swank bar bought it and turned it into this speakeasy sort of thing. I moonlight there sometimes, bartending."

"Why do you sound as though you belong in an American sitcom?" I grumbled, failing to see the point.

"Thanks!" Baz said, as ever completely oblivious to any attempt at an insult, veiled or otherwise. Not that I had a problem with American sitcoms; Yolanda was very fond of them, and she often made Agravane and I watch them with her after work. I usually had to have the plot explained to me slowly.

"Anyways, I was thinking we should go. I've got a shift tonight, and maybe you can meet up with some of my friends. You'd like them. They're posh, like you."

"Thank you?" I had met Baz's friends in the past, and rarely got along with them. Of course, most of them were criminals of one sort or another, and very few wanted anything to do with marketing.

"Yeah, no problem. Then you can tell me more about why you're here!" Baz bounced up from the table with all the energy of a kitten and vanished into the rest of the house, presumably to change into something not plaid or striped. I didn't even get a chance to tell him that I was here because he had gotten mixed up with the wrong sort of people and was potentially going to be responsible for starting the magical apocalypse.

On second thought, perhaps it would be better if I accompanied my wayward cousin to this swank bar, whatever that meant.

3

HOME TOWN

When Baz emerged about twenty minutes later, I was fairly certain that his change of clothes was not an improvement. For one, they were wrinkled like they'd been picked up off his floor with little consideration for whether they were clean or not. And then there was the fact that he was wearing a band t-shirt from some band I'd never heard of and a pair of chinos that were two inches too short.

"Does your shirt say Tiny Dinosaurs With Phasers?" I asked, staring at the strange drawing of a t-rex holding some sort of space gun. Baz grinned and looked down at his shirt.

"Yeah, they're only the greatest punk band ever!" he said. Then, he clapped me on the shoulder again and practically skipped to the door. "I knew you'd understand."

I decided that discretion was the better part of valour and kept my mouth shut. My mother was nowhere in sight, so I just followed Baz out the door and didn't bother leaving a note to say where I was going. I did, however, liberate some cash from her desk drawer as Life and Death had so graciously sent me off with only my phone in my pocket and the clothes I was wearing.

Figures.

Baz kept up a fairly constant stream of chatter as we walked to this bar. I listened with half-an-ear and mostly just took in the familiar streets. The same sorts of cars were parked here, and the buildings looked exactly as they had before I left. London was an unusual town; by all accounts, a very modern city with its population on the pulse of the trends in the world, but it didn't often change much. It was full of people who preferred to look at their phones rather than strike up a conversation, but you also didn't feel looked down on by the other people walking around. Everyone and anyone lived there, and you could meet people with any background.

It was a place I had once proudly called home. Now, it just felt like any other city in the mortal realms. Okay, except Chicago. Chicago would always have its own special memories of being attacked by pianos and long-dead gangsters bent on returning to life. I had mixed feelings about Chicago. Most of them bad feelings, even without full emotional capacity.

But many of the other places I'd been to in the mortal realms in the last couple of years had this sort of universal feeling to it. People were trying very hard to just get on with their lives, and often I was there to get in their way. London no longer felt like home. Half the streets Baz and I were walking felt unfamiliar, as if I'd not once fled from a dog in that alley, or flirted with my first girlfriend in the coffee shop there.

"Hey, man," Baz said. "You seem a little quiet. Things okay?"

I looked at him, knowing that I should be feeling something right then, but feeling very little in actuality. Baz was my cousin, but he was also one of the few people in the family that didn't bother conforming to expectations. As a result, we'd gotten up to a lot of shenanigans in our youth. Granted, most of my actions involved cleaning up after Baz's brand of shenanigans. Now, he was just a means to an end, another task to tidy up before I could go home and sleep.

Part of me wondered if that was just a bit sad.

"I'm fine," I said calmly. "I don't feel things normally since losing my soul. A side effect."

Baz winced and shook his head. "That's rough. I mean, you get to come home for the first time since you died—"

"I didn't die," I pointed out.

"Since you basically died," Baz retorted. "You come home and you can't even be happy to be here. No wonder Aunt Teresa is all weird."

"She doesn't seem weird," I said, quirking a brow.

"She didn't even hug you," Baz said. "That seems weird."

I nodded. "Ah, you must not have lived with her for

long. She does not hug. I thought her reactions today seemed to be displaying rather a lot of feeling, actually."

Baz shot me a sidelong look that was halfway disturbed. He shook his head and ran a hand through his hair, making it stand up on end. A couple of girls probably just in university giggled quietly as he did before ducking into a corner shop and staring out the window. This was a fairly normal occurrence for Baz, so I ignored it.

"Aunt Teresa is never like that with me. She usually complains a bunch, loudly, but it comes from a good place. You have a seriously messed up life," he said.

"This is an accurate statement," I agreed. I doubted we were referring to the same things to define my "messed up" life.

Baz stopped suddenly, standing up straighter and looking at me with a wide grin on his face. He gestured to a building that looked almost like all the other buildings on the street. It had a stone facade that was slightly grimy near the bottom, tall windows covered by thick velvet curtains on the inside, a green-painted door, and a large sign dangling from a steel rod that read: Magic Potions Bar. It reeked of otherworldliness.

Sebastian sat up straight deep inside me and gave me a frown. I found I couldn't disagree with that assessment. This was obviously not a good situation. Still, as I was meant to be getting my cousin out of a not good situation, I figured we were in the right place.

I just hoped that none of the magical denizens of

Elsewhere were in there. I really hoped that it was just a silly human fondness for magic and magic-related things that came out of the Harry Potter craze. I hoped that things weren't about to get worse.

Baz opened the door and gestured me in. Things, then, got worse.

The first thing I noticed weren't the art deco style lights or the vintage style furniture, the art on the walls that was definitely from the twenties, or even the fact that the bar had a wonderfully shiny coffee machine next to their large array of alcohols—okay, I will admit to noticing the coffee machine—but the clientele. Firstly, they were all dressed well. In my three-piece suit that I'd had tailored by a pair of craft elves, with its minuscule pinstripes, the black silk brocade waistcoat and a bright blue pocket square, of a quality that could not be found in the mortal realms, I fit in perfectly.

Baz, on the other hand, stuck out like a sore thumb in his strange t-shirt. He also stuck out because he was very much human, and these people were very much not.

I'd come across a few places like this in my time working for Death. They were places in the normal world that catered to beings whose nature was magical or legendary or immortal, or all three. They were usually places of business, where Fae or vampires, werewolves and other bloodshifters, dryads, naiads, trolls, ogres and the like could all gather and not have to worry about keeping up guises or glamours for the puny little humans who wandered around the mortal realms. These places usually had one foot in Elsewhere, the magical realm that existed separate from the mortal realms, and they were very dangerous for the uninitiated.

Humans were, for most of these creatures, both prey and predator. On their own, humans were extremely fragile. We could be cut with less than a pound of pressure, our insides were very squishy, we had no propensity for magic or supernatural healing, and we were often very oblivious to the magical side of things. Now, that being said, humans rarely played by the rules that most creatures of Elsewhere followed. We were crafty and cruel and en masse could take on just about anything thrown our way. We were resilient and very afraid of things that we did not understand.

Yolanda and Agravane often explained to me that I was the exception rather than the rule, because while I got screamy and annoyed when things tried to kill me, I didn't take it personally. And I worked for Death, which gave me added protection and awareness.

The Magic Potions Bar was full of beings that I could tell at a glance were the magical equivalent of Bad News. In the corner were two creatures with vertical slitted eyes and a smattering of scales across their faces that were likely related to dragons or demons. They watched Baz and me with that stillness of predators. A hunched figure sitting on a stool at the bar was shrouded in rags and had hair that looked as though it was made from steel wool, but I had no doubt that she was a witch or something equally powerful. There were three Fae of some sort in the corner opposite the reptile people and the shadows that seemed to hover over the party sitting at a table beneath a probably priceless Picasso hid a fair amount of power.

If the sheer number of highly dangerous beings in the room wasn't problematic enough, I recognised the woman leaning against the corner of the bar with an expression of both distaste and boredom written very clearly across her stunningly beautiful face.

Baz didn't bother introducing me around, he just waved enthusiastically to the current bartender—a man that looked to be entirely made of water, complete with tiny goldfish swimming beneath his skin—before slipping into the back and leaving me to fend for myself. I sat at the bar beside the woman.

"Hello, Mercy," I said, trying to put a smile on my face. I think I failed, though.

Mercy was an assassin that belonged to the Order of Silence, an organisation dedicated to preserving the balance of the universe, namely between Life and Death. She was an aurai, like Agravane, only more of the immortal sort than my junior marketing agent, given that she actively embodied the concept of Mercy. She was tall, graceful, with dark skin and hair that today looked like the colour of cinnamon bark. She also more or less loathed me.

"Cal Thorpe," Mercy said, frowning. "I should have known that you would show up at some point."

"Really?" I asked, a sliver of curiosity snaking up

my spine. I ordered a gin and tonic from the bartender, who gave me a forlorn look and sulked through the process of making my drink. I should have asked for coffee. "Why would you say that?"

Mercy tapped her fingertips on the polished wood of the bar once, enough to let me know that she was rattled by my presence. "Because just when I think things are going well, you seem to arrive and ruin my existence."

I frowned, the expression feeling far more successful than my attempt at smiling. "I haven't seen you since Death's family reunion, and we didn't even converse, then. The last time we interacted was when your Order had me impaled on a stalagmite and preparing for my demise. Which didn't work, need I remind you?"

Mercy scowled and the varnish of the wood cracked beneath her fingers. "You...you...you infuriate me! You made me look like a fool before the head of my Order and you are directly responsible for Justice's death."

"That was not my fault," I protested flatly. The bartender placed my drink before me and I did my best to thank him politely. He seemed distinctly distraught by this and stomped to the other end of the bar.

"He's upset because of your drink order," Mercy explained. "He doesn't like making normal drinks that you can buy in any bar in London."

"Well, I've never been here before, and it's been

years since I've been to London, let alone had a proper gin and tonic," I grumbled, sipping at my drink. It was perfect, and I felt a tiny piece of tension leave my shoulders. Sebastian writhed inside me with a pleased murmur. Apparently my Reaper half liked gin and tonic.

Mercy studied me for a moment, her gaze hard and unyielding. I expected no less from her, frankly. "You are nothing more than a foolish human, and yet you somehow could not die. You somehow stood between Life and Death and achieved what I have been working towards since my initiation into the Order."

I raised a finger. "Point of contention, when your Order had me impaled, that was simply because Death accidentally replaced my lifeforce with my soul. He fixed that."

Mercy brightened almost immediately, the change so striking that she seemed almost to glow. "It was a mistake?!"

"Yes," I said.

"Then you can die." I wasn't sure I liked the slightly gleeful tone in her voice at that.

"No," I said, taking another sip of my drink. "Shortly afterwards, Death lost my soul during the height of the Renaissance—it's a long story—and I developed into a Reaper."

If I thought I had shocked Mercy before, now she looked as though the ground had dropped away from beneath her feet. Her eyes widened, her mouth dropped, and she stopped breathing. "No," she said on a breath, utter devastation in her voice. "No, it's not possible."

I studied her for a moment, realising after a few seconds that I had probably made things worse. Mercy wanted to be the perfect example of balance between Life and Death; it was pretty much the entire point of her Order and she wholeheartedly believed in what she did to achieve that goal. Then, like some bumbling idiot, I waltz in and announce that I have lost my soul, cannot die, and am a Reaper whose entire purpose is to stand between Life and Death.

"I'm sorry," I said, actually feeling the truth in my words resonate. "I didn't know."

"Reapers haven't been seen in centuries," Mercy whispered. "I was trying so hard and then you just... why are you here, Cal?"

Just then, Baz stepped out of the back room and behind the bar, clapping the watery bartender on the shoulder and getting a grimace in return. I nodded towards him. "He's my cousin. I was sent here to stop him from doing something...bad, I think. Neither Life nor Death explained much about the situation, except that it involved the natural order of the mortal realms and if I didn't intervene, then it would be potentially catastrophic."

Mercy let out a brittle laugh that drew Baz's attention. He gave me a look of consternation. I ignored it and took another sip of my gin and tonic.

"I was sent by the Order for much the same

reason," Mercy said. "Only, I was to correct the potential imbalance by any means necessary."

I said nothing, the highly rational part of my brain that often led the charge these days, since I wasn't feeling much, figuring out the answer with little difficulty. "You're going to kill Baz," I said.

Mercy nodded. "If I cannot solve the imbalance any other way, then yes. He will die."

Sebastian, more awake than usual since I started drinking the gin and tonic, sat up straighter and opened both eyes wide, focusing all its attention on Mercy. While it wasn't precisely an emotional response, it was also not a purely logical one, either. It was like I had stuck my finger into an electrical socket and was feeling all the energy surge through me without any of the fear of causing damage or pain or dying.

Mercy sucked in a sharp breath. "What is *that*?" she hissed.

I was surprised that she could even see or sense Sebastian, since there was, as far as I could tell, no outward sign of my Reaper abilities. Perhaps it was because she was more closely attuned to such things, being hyper-aware of the balance, or perhaps it was just because she was an assassin herself. Either way, it forced me to blink, startling Sebastian out of snarly-mode.

"That is Sebastian," I said in a low voice. "My Reaper half."

This time, the ever-graceful, incredibly beautiful

assassin spluttered and looked for all the world like someone who had just been slapped on live television. I had been watching far too many sitcoms and soap operas with Yolanda and Agravane.

"You gave your Reaper abilities a name." Mercy laughed unsteadily. "This is even more of a mess than I thought. All this time in seclusion at the Order, trying to better understand, and I just had to pop into a mortal realm bar to have the mysteries of the universe thrust in my face. I think I hate you Cal."

I nodded. "I understand. Now that we've gotten that out of the way, perhaps you would like to enlighten me on just what sort of situation my cousin has gotten himself involved in? Death mentioned something about Dragonwort, and the magical rule here. I wasn't really listening; Life had nearly spilled my coffee."

Mercy took three deep breaths, likely considering several ways she could go about ending my life. It wouldn't take, as ever, but I could see that she was slightly more stable after her breathing exercise, so I didn't say anything. Then, she nodded ever so slightly towards the table of shadows by the wall. "Do you see them?"

"The things hiding in darkness? Yes, I see them. Sort of." I couldn't actually make out many details, but I could see enough to get a sense of glowing eyes and sharp claws and a deep power that could shake the foundations of the world if annoyed.

"Those are the giants, rulers of Beneath," Mercy

said. She turned away from them after a moment, as if uninterested by whatever she saw there. I noted, though, a glimmer of something in her eye, and she clutched at the bar again, her fingers tracing over the cracked varnish.

"I would pretend to know what that means, but I think I should ask, instead," I replied. Sebastian turned over inside me and cast a glance through lidded eye at the beings. It turned its attention back on Mercy, finding her the more interesting quarry. She bared her teeth at me.

"Are you ignorant in everything?" Mercy snapped. "The mortal realms are divided into two: Above and Beneath."

"Above and Beneath what? The ground?" I asked, doing my best to keep my tone carefully casual, so as not to offend. I needed this information for whatever it was that Life and Death had sent me for. A niggling thought in the back of my mind had me frowning into my drink. Had Life sent Mercy here to give me the answers I needed? She had hinted at something.

"Sometimes, yes. It is not always so easy." Mercy shook her head. "They are metaphorical concepts as much as literal ones. The Goblin Market belongs Beneath, though it exists beside the world. The burrowing creatures who live in mountains and rivers often obey those Above. The creatures of Elsewhere that choose to walk here must pick a side. Most that you see, the Fae, the vampires, those that walk amongst humans in secret and shadow? They technically obey the rulers of Above. But the influence of Beneath is growing. In part due to your cousin."

I nodded, acting like I understood what was being said. Frankly, I was still caught up on the whole up, down, above, beneath thing. In my logical state, I was not often very good at metaphor. "Okay, so the power is divided. Got it. If the rulers of Beneath manage to replace the rulers of Above...?"

Mercy gave a dark chuckle, the one that reminded me why she was an assassin. "The world as you know it will end. And it will end in fire."

4
____

THE WAY BACK HOME

"*D*o you take lessons on how to be melodramatic in your Order of Silence? Because you are really doing exceptionally well."

Mercy's jaw dropped. "Are you being *sarcastic*?"

I shrugged. "It's one of the few emotion-like things that I can do on a regular basis, despite being soulless. Death assures me that it is actually a good thing, but Yolanda isn't quite so sure."

At this point in our discussion about potential ways that the world could fall into tiny little pieces, my cousin decided to interrupt. He put on his charmer's grin for Mercy, who sniffed disdainfully. "I see you've met my cousin, Cal. He's usually much better at conversation."

Mercy fixed me with a look I couldn't quite decipher. I stared blankly back. "I'm sure it's fine," she said through gritted teeth.

Baz straightened and clapped his hands together.

"Great! So, I'm Basil, but everyone calls me Baz. It is an absolute pleasure to meet you. I'm your bartender here at Magic Potions. So, can I whip you up something special?"

Mercy blinked at Baz, then looked between him and me, the most blatant confusion on her face. I waited for Baz to repeat himself, but he just stood there with his smile painted on, waiting for an answer. I decided to take pity on him.

"Baz, this is Mercy," I said, waving my hand in introduction. "I told you about her earlier."

Baz's eyes grew comically large and the charming grin slipped off his face into another oblivion. Now he was the one looking between Mercy and myself, obviously confused. "Mercy the assassin, Mercy?" he breathed.

"I am an agent of *balance*," Mercy grumbled.

"Yes," I said, to both of them. "She has come to help with, ah, things."

Baz leaned closer. "Things?"

How does one explain to a family member that they might be responsible for starting the apocalypse? I just nodded. "Yes. Things. Now, explain to me how exactly you got this job. I mean, you *do* know what this place is, don't you?"

Frankly, it would not have surprised me to learn that Baz had absolutely no idea where he was working. Humans who do not wish to see the truth rarely do. I've met a few people who can stare magical beings in the face and pretend that they never existed. I've also met a few people who could look obliquely at anything remotely magical and figure things out on their own. I used to belong to the slightly-more-oblivious category. Yolanda assured me I had adapted well. Agravane usually laughed when she said that.

Baz shrugged. "Sure. I mean, you don't honestly think that I would have accepted your story so easily if I didn't, right? It is a little farfetched. Even for magic."

I blinked. Frowned. Considered my almost-empty gin and tonic. To please Sebastian, I finished it off. "A coffee, please," I said, sliding the empty glass to Baz.

"Seriously, Cal?" Mercy asked with a very obvious eye-roll. "You expected him to believe your story without proof?"

"Well, yes," I said. "As the only way to prove such a thing would be to die, and I would prefer to avoid that. It does mess up my clothes a bit. And it tends to hurt."

Baz snorted. "No, I knew you were telling the truth. I don't know about Aunt Teresa, but I understand. I mean, I work here, and if I didn't know what was going on I would have really freaked out. I mean, I *did* freak out when I first found out—"

"And how was that, exactly?" I asked. I did my best not to sound demanding or threatening, but my eyes narrowed and I'm fairly certain that Sebastian growled. Baz just chuckled. The shrouded hag waved him over and he pushed away to make her a drink, and to get my coffee. When he returned, I snatched at the mug and took a desperate sip, all thoughts of interrogating my cousin gone. I winced.

"You call this coffee?" I grumbled.

"That's what you get for ordering coffee in a bar."

I sniffed and took another sip of the coffee; sub par drink or not, it was coffee, and I wasn't going to give it up. Not when my normal stash of brownie made coffee was who knows how many days away.

"Alright," I said, lowering the mug to the bar. "Why don't you tell me what happened. How did you get your job here?"

Baz grinned like a little kid and leaned his elbows on the bar. "Okay, so it was like this. I was walking home from the auto shop, you know where I used to work?"

"Yes," I said drily, "the auto shop that tore apart stolen vehicles and sold the parts."

Baz frowned. "I was hoping you wouldn't remember that bit."

I waved my hand. "Ignoring previous criminal activities, got it. Moving on."

"Anyways," Baz grumbled, giving me a pointed look. I could have told him such things were wasted on me when I had no concept of my own emotions, let alone anyone else's. I didn't, instead pretending to ignore the look entirely. "I was walking home from work and went through the park. It was dinner time, maybe, dark, but I could still see. Well, this guy comes barrelling along, practically screaming about how he shot someone and just needed some money. He runs into me, drops a gun, and runs away. Well, I'm not just going to stand there and leave a gun for anyone to find, so I pick it up."

The story was strangely familiar, like hearing about an event from someone else's perspective when you had been standing on the opposite side of the room. I frowned. "You didn't call the police?"

Baz snorted. "Seriously, Cal? I worked at a chop shop. I wasn't dumb enough to call the police, not after I picked it *up*. Guns are hard enough to get as it is, without handing the rozzers one with my fingerprints on it. No, I didn't call the police."

Mercy shot me a look. "Your cousin does have a point. This country is rather harsh on guns."

I sighed. "I am *aware* of that."

"So I had this gun, and it was dark, and some guy had just been shot in the park. I started heading in the opposite direction, hoping to avoid any police or bystanders or stuff, so I walked through the trees. I mean, you know the park, Cal, it's hardly a *forest*. But I was going through the trees, and suddenly there was this *wolf*! Not some dog, an actual wolf!" Baz held up his hands to emphasise his point, drawing the attention of the hag and the Fae in the bar. I hissed under my breath.

"Do try to be subtle, Baz! We don't need the whole magical community knowing what's going on."

Baz shrugged apologetically and picked up a rag, wiping down the counters. After the general interest subsided, he started talking again, only slightly lower in volume. "So this wolf stars coming towards me. I ran. The wolf ran faster. It was just about on me when I pulled out the gun and shot it. Bam! Right in the chest. It goes down and then turns into a person. Like, an actual human being."

Mercy and I exchanged a glance. "Werewolf," I said. She nodded. I hadn't had any personal dealings with werewolves, as they tended to stick to themselves. I knew there was a fairly large presence in the Americas, but they were all over, as were other blood-based magic shifters.

"Yeah," Baz said, nodding. "A freaking werewolf, right in the middle of London. Talk about your movie situations. Alright, so I'm freaking out, but before I can even scream, these things show up. Like from the ground, show up. They're all super scary shadowy figures with glowing eyes and they just *look* at me."

I glanced over my shoulder at the table of shadowy figures, the giants as Mercy described them. They don't look like giants to me, but as I hadn't actually met a giant, I wasn't going to point that out. There were all sorts of guises a creature could wear.

Baz caught the line of my gaze and thumped the bar. I turned back to glare at him. "Yeah, those guys. Anyways, one of them starts talking and I figure I'm done for it. No, they *thank* me! Say that the wolf was guarding one of the entrances to their homes, trying to keep them locked up, and I freed them. Asked me if I wanted a job, delivering messages, running errands. Said I was obviously a discerning human, obviously meant for great things. I figured, hey, if they pay me, why not. Besides, I like doing good, and these guys had been locked up for so long they weren't really comfortable out in the world. I said I'd help them out. Started running packages, delivering messages, that sort of thing. Eventually, they found me this job and here I am! Been here for about six months. You know, it's a good gig, Cal. Helping them, learning about all the cool stuff that really goes on in the world. It's a nice job."

I had so very many questions, not the least of which was whether my cousin was an idiot. He had good intentions, but he very rarely asked whether something was right or not. He just did things and worried about the consequences later. Helping out these giants, these rulers of Beneath, would have seemed very cool to him, and he wouldn't have once asked why they were "locked up." Granted, even if he had, Baz was the sort to believe what was told to him.

"Six months, huh?" I asked, swirling my coffee in my mug. "And when did this whole thing first happen?"

Baz considered, tilting his head. "Maybe two years? Maybe a little more?"

I lowered my head to the bar and tried very hard not to groan out loud. Two years or so. Two years or so ago, I had been shot in a park and then hired by Death. I would bet my glasses that the gun that shot me was what got Baz into this situation. Life was too fond of coincidence for anything else.

"Okay, next question," I said, lifting my head and

ignoring the concerned looks from Baz and Mercy. "Delivering packages. What sort of packages?"

Now, Baz did look a little uncomfortable. "Ah, well, I asked once. They said it was drugs of some sort."

I lowered my head to the bar again. "Of course it was."

"Hey, I protested, said I wasn't really okay with that, but they said it was for their friends, and that it wasn't problematic like most of the human drugs. It was more like...magical supplements. To make you stronger, healthier, that sort of thing."

Mercy snorted in a very unladylike way, practically sneering at Baz. "You are more naive than Cal, which I had thought impossible."

"Hey," I snapped, lifting my head. "Don't talk to my cousin like that."

Mercy lifted one shoulder and sniffed. "I speak truth. It is more merciful to be aware of one's faults rather than suffering evermore."

"That's debatable," I retorted. "And besides, if anyone is going to tell him off, it will be me. For that matter, what are you still doing here?"

"I told you, I was sent here by the Order of Silence. Whether you were sent for the same reason is completely irrelevant. I will see this through to the end." I could tell she would be just fine using whatever means necessary on that front, and I wanted none of it. Baz was often painfully naive, or simply not so good on the right versus wrong scale, but he did not deserve to die.

I pushed my glasses up my nose and sat up straighter, glaring at Mercy with all the force of my Reaper abilities behind the look, Sebastian sitting at attention within me. "I cannot control you," I said, voice low, "but remember, Mercy, that I am not as fragile as you. We will do this *my* way, and that means you will do nothing to hurt my family."

Mercy narrowed her eyes at me. Whatever abilities she had that could sense Sebastian must have told her that I was quite serious, because she gave one tense nod and looked away. As far as battles of dominance were concerned, I had won. She hated me for it, but that was nothing new.

When I turned to look at Baz, though, I saw something in my cousin's eyes that I had never seen before. Fear. This was startling enough to shock my Reaper abilities back into place and I just finished off my coffee.

"Baz, we will have a talk later about drugs and not getting involved in things beyond your ken. For now, though, how about you introduce me to your new associates."

Baz took my empty mug and put it in the sink behind the bar, running the rag over the wood and then tossing it down, too. He nodded. "Alright, Cal," he said, a tired tone in his voice. Inwardly, I groaned. Baz was cheerful a good ninety percent of the time, but when he decided that the world was treating him wrong, he could be a master of the sulks and the despondent, pointed looks. My mother swore that he got it from his mother, who had pouted her way into prosperity, but I thought that might have been a bit much. Baz's mum was more whiny; Baz just had a hard time with the world taking him seriously.

"Hey," I said. "It's going to be alright."

"Sure, Cal," Baz said with a half-smile. It would have to do.

He stepped out from behind the bar and walked over to the table with the shadowy figures. I followed, Mercy at my shoulder. Baz's posture changed as he walked, shoulders straightening and that same charming smile of his lighting up his features. There was a reason why people liked Baz so much, after all. He was good with people. Mostly.

"Good evening," Baz said, a hint of extra formality in his voice. "I brought someone to meet you. This is my cousin, Cal—"

"We do not want introductions," a voice slithered from the shadows. As I got closer to the table, I could see the beings there more clearly. The one that spoke was in the form of a man with skin the colour of twilight blue, a beard of white hair covering his chin and eyes that were reptilian yellow. He wore a suit that was nice enough to rival Death's sartorial excellence— no matter how I tried, Death would not give me the name of his tailor—and presided over the table like a CEO certain of his authority.

Despite all of that, though, he did not look to be any taller than me, and I couldn't quite figure out why

Mercy had called him, and the others at the table, a giant.

"You will want this introduction," Mercy said, her voice silky smooth and her bearing full of immortal grace and predatory power.

"Yeah, I mean, Cal looks a little stiff, but he's a nice guy," Baz put in. I shot him a look, confusion trickling up my spine. Stiff? Was it because of my suit? I liked suits. They were very comfortable. And it certainly wasn't in reference to my posture. Agravane had complained numerous times during our attempted training sessions that I had just enough of a slouch to throw off the techniques that he was trying to teach.

The giant waved his hand dismissively. "Go away, aurai. We have enough humans at our disposal. We don't need another. Certainly not simply because he is family to a servant."

Baz winced at that, but said nothing, none of his usual spunk standing up to the casual dismissal by the giant. I began to understand how it was that he had gotten entangled in this mess. After the initial flattery for having freed them, I imagine that they simply crushed Baz under their blue thumbs and demanded he do as they ask. Like I said, humans are fragile.

"Don't talk to my cousin that way," I said, voice low. I was fairly used to people underestimating me because I was human, but I also had some extra advantages, such as the fact that I worked for Death, who was more or less one of the heaviest hitters in the entirety of the magical community. I could handle people sneering at me and generally causing me trouble. I didn't like it when they did the same to my friends, or my family.

The giant grinned slowly at me, showing all his teeth, like some weird toothpaste commercial. "Such *insolence* from an insignificant speck. Iago, kill him."

Another one of the giants, this one with the physique of a dancer and the clothes of some eighteenth century pirate, white hair down to his shoulders, moved from his chair so fluidly that I immediately wondered if he would be willing to help with some of my marketing campaigns for the coffee I was pushing. Then, he grabbed my head and snapped my neck with that same fluidity that I decided I really shouldn't bother.

As far as deaths go, that one was far swifter than many I had experienced. It was also far less painful than my usual experiences with people trying to get rid of me, so I recovered fast enough that I didn't even fall to the floor. My vision just flashed with a familiar whiteness and I was back to normal, blinking and shifting my shoulders to get rid of the strangeness of having my neck rotated into an abnormal position.

Baz's mouth dropped open and I was fairly certain he was about to scream. I decided to prevent that, since his screams were really hard on the ears.

"Well, that's almost better than a chiropractor," I said, shaking my head from side to side, as if testing out my muscles. "Though, I think your technique could use some work."

Iago stood there, frozen, his eyes wide. He was shoved aside by the angry CEO giant, who glowered down at me, despite being my height. "What trickery is this?" he roared, setting the rafters to shaking.

I responded by grinning slowly at him, mocking his earlier swagger. "No trick," I said. "It was rather rude on your part to go attacking people with no provocation. Don't guest laws prohibit such things?"

Mercy sucked in a breath, as if I had done something incredibly stupid. This would not have surprised me; I was decently capable at doing incredibly stupid things without much effort. This, though, was intentional. I had invoked guest laws, which were one of the more stringent guidelines for beings of the magical sort. They were the things that kept many of the highly dangerous beings from going to war over tiny offenses, like killing your neighbours. While they did rely on actually being a guest in a being's domain, I rather assumed that these giants had claimed the bar for that. Why else would they have gotten Baz a job there?

The giant narrowed his eyes at me. "Who are you?"

"This is my cousin, Cal," Baz put in, once more wearing his charming grin, though he looked a little pale, and he kept glancing over at me as if I was about to keel over. I gave a little wave.

"Hello," I said.

The giant narrowed his eyes at Baz, then looked over at me and finally at Iago, who was standing silently off to the side, flexing his fingers. "Very well then. You are not so useless as you seem, Basil," the giant said. He gestured to the table. "Cal, sit. I believe that we have some things to discuss."

I shrugged and gestured to Mercy, even going so far as to hold out a chair for her. She glared at me, but sat, her shoulders back and her movements precise. "This is my friend, Mercy," I said, offering no more introduction than that. Iago sat at Mercy's other side, nodding to her. She ignored him.

"Friend? Cal, you know we are so much more than that," Mercy said, reaching out to tug me into the unoccupied chair beside her. I tripped and fell into the seat, unbalanced enough for Mercy to snake her arm through mine and give me a warning squeeze on the arm. I gave a weak smile.

The leader of the giants took his place at the table and waved a dismissive hand to Baz. "Drinks, all around!" he growled. Baz didn't hesitate, vanishing behind the bar to go get us drinks. He returned a moment later with various glasses of alcohol, a gin and tonic placed directly in front of me.

The giant lifted his glass of some sort of whiskey or bourbon or something. "Then, a welcome! To Cal and his girlfriend, Mercy, a greeting and alliance!"

I coughed halfway through my sip of the drink and shot a glance at Mercy. She was my what now?

5

CAN'T GO HOME

I was fairly certain I had missed some important subtext or something. I'd been told—mostly by Agravane—that my inability to feel emotions properly was highly problematic when dealing with people who actually did feel emotions. I tended to miss important social cues and had caused offense on more than one occasion.

I hadn't, though, missed knowing that someone was my girlfriend, even in such unusual circumstances as these. Logically, I knew that Mercy was pretending in order to maintain a low profile, and that I should just simply play along and let her tell me about her schemes later, when we weren't dealing with highly dangerous individuals. I also couldn't get it out of my head.

"I am Tiberius, lord of Beneath and giant," the CEO said, clasping a fist to his chest. This provided enough distraction that I stopped gaping at Mercy and instead turned my confusion to this Tiberius.

"You don't *look* like a giant. I mean, we're the same height and I am average, for a human," I said, frowning. Mercy squeezed my arm in what I am fairly certain was meant to be a warning gesture. I ignored her.

Tiberius blinked at me, then looked to Mercy and back to me. Finally, he started laughing, the sound loud enough to shake the rafters. "You are most *amusing*, Cal. You think this is our full form, that we would concentrate all our powers in one vessel and not shatter the foundations of the world? No, we sleep, but part of our dreams break off and allow us to commune with the world. It is the only way, to keep the dwellers alive."

I sipped at my gin and tonic, still confused but in a different direction. Mercy squeezed my arm harder. I looked at her hand, then up at her. She leaned in close, her mouth brushing my ear. It was very ticklish. "Ask questions later, Cal. We have a job to do."

That was all very well and good, but I honestly had no idea what I was even meant to be *doing* here. Life and Death had not been very clear, and I was pretty sure that Baz was not going to be much help. Instead of asking questions, though, I took another sip of the gin and tonic and felt Sebastian settle into a sort of watchful interest. Mercy nodded and released some of the pressure on my arm.

"So, uh, Baz said that you were the people to meet," I started, not entirely sure how to actually ask these people whether they were trying to start a war or upset the apparently precarious balance of the mortal realms. In these sorts of circumstances, people usually just told me their plans and I did my best to foil them.

It struck me that I was perhaps overly fortunate in my past jobs.

"Indeed," Tiberius said with a sly look. "Your cousin has been a great friend to us. He was the one who freed us from our prison."

"You were imprisoned?" I asked. I attempted to put an appropriate amount of shock into the words, but Mercy gave a slight cough, which was often an indication that I had overdone it a bit. I took another sip of my drink. "I will admit that I have not been well informed of the, ah, magical goings-on of the mortal realms. My work has mostly involved denizens of Elsewhere."

Iago exchanged a glance with Tiberius, who then leaned forwards with a very interested gleam in his eye. Frankly, this whole conversation was not going particularly well for me. "You work in Elsewhere, eh? My, my, Basil does have interesting familial connections indeed."

As Mercy wasn't coughing in my ear, nor was she squeezing my arm until my fingers threatened to fall off, I decided to continue. I pulled out my phone and opened the social media app favoured in Elsewhere. At the top of the page was one of my better campaign pictures for the coffee I was marketing. I handed it over, sitting up straighter.

Tiberius took the phone in his hands as if he was unfamiliar with the device. He looked at it closely, frowning, then handed it over to Iago. Tiberius smoothed the white hair of his beard. "You...market coffee?"

I nodded eagerly. "It is the best coffee *ever*. I found it on a trip through the Goblin Market while I was searching for the Iron Witch, and the brownie who made it agreed to give me a lifetime supply in exchange for doing marketing for them. I have tried all the varieties so far, and I think the dark roast is probably the best, though the medium roast with a hint of cinnamon is really good, too. And next month, I'm going to see about getting them involved in a coffee subscription box so that our market saturation will increase and—"

Mercy placed a hand over my mouth. "Cal is Death's personal marketing agent, though he takes on other jobs occasionally."

The giants stared at me with the sort of expression one usually reserves for the truly strange or astonishing, such as someone going to the shops in footie pajamas. "Truly?" Tiberius asked.

I nodded. "Yes, I do work for Death, though he allows me to contract out."

The giants seemed to swell in size, until they were leaning over me in an overbearing manner. I wondered vaguely if I was meant to feel threatened by such a display of power. To me, it seemed that the wide grins negated that potential. "Well, well, how truly fortuitous," Tiberius purred, the sound more like an avalanche than a house cat. "Cal, I think we are going to be good friends."

"Oh, that's nice," I said.

"Tell me, what do you know about the Beneath?"

"It's not the same as below?" I shrugged. "In most thesauruses, the words are noted as synonyms, but generally I have found that the differences in meaning are slight and—"

Tiberius waved a dismissive hand. He quirked an eyebrow at Mercy. "Is your boyfriend always this literal?"

Mercy nodded. "It's part of his charm. Cal is extremely capable, but you have to spell out what you want from him quite clearly. Otherwise, you get pulled into long discussions of the nature of c-o-f-f-e-e."

"I can spell, you know," I sniffed. Mercy chuckled, the sound dark and promising extreme amounts of danger. At this point, Baz sidled up to the table, looking a little nervous and tugging at his Tiny Dinosaurs With Phasers shirt.

"Can I get you anything else?" he asked, removing my empty gin and tonic glass. "Something to eat, perhaps?"

I blinked. "I thought this was a bar. They serve food here?"

"Most bars serve food these days, Cal," Baz said with a smile, like I was five. I ignored the slight; my cousin had been arguing about my relative maturity for years. I often returned the favour with equal vigour, at least when I cared about such things.

"We need nothing," Tiberius said with a growl to his voice, completely different from the pleased sound he had made when learning about my profession. "Return to your place."

I narrowed my eyes. "Hold on a minute," I said, grabbing Baz's wrist to keep him from slinking away. "My cousin is not some sort of servant."

"Cal, really, it's not a big deal," Baz argued. "It's my job. I don't need—"

"It is a big deal," I said. "You may be a bartender, but that's not an excuse to treat you like...like..."

"Like a fragile human in a world of predators?" Mercy asked, not unkindly. She was simply being merciful, to both Baz and me, reminding me that while my cousin was caught up in something decidedly magical in nature, he didn't actually have any of the advantages I had. I frowned deeper, Sebastian writhing inside me, a growl inches away from the surface.

"Cal, just let it go," Baz breathed. I looked at Baz, really looked at him, and saw the way his eyes darted to Tiberius and then to the floor, his mouth open slightly and a distinct hitch to his breath. Fear.

Logically, I knew that I should do as Baz asked. I was intervening on his behalf, after all, doing my best to get him out of whatever situation he'd gotten himself into. Delivering Dragonwort, acting at the beck and call of giants who, by all indications, were pretty powerful beings. Relegated to the role of insignificant speck. I could get Baz out of this, let him go back to living a relatively normal life. Whatever scars, physical or emotional, would be his to deal with them, but at least he would have the chance to do just that, instead of being caught up in world-changing events.

One of the downsides of my particular condition—Phantom Soul Syndrome, Death called it—was that, while I acted logically ninety percent of the time, there were a few circumstances where such a thing was just not possible. Mostly, the uncontrollable emotions surrounded coffee. But Baz was family, and family was more important than coffee.

"No," I said, a definitive growl to my voice. "It is *not* okay. Baz is not just some human. He's intelligent and capable and you are treating him like he's nothing."

"Iago here could snap his neck with no effort at all," Tiberius said, narrowing his eyes at me. "You are useful, Cal, but he is not. In fact, he's already served his purpose. I kept him around for sentiment, as he did free us from our prison, intentionally or not, but servants are replaceable. You would do well to keep on our good side, or your cousin will pay the price."

"*Cal,*" Mercy hissed, her tone moving towards actual fury. She wanted me to keep quiet. To keep my head down and let these giants reveal their plans to me so I could stop them. So she could stop them. Preserve the balance and all that. It wasn't going to happen.

I stood from the chair, making it scrape across the floor in a hugely loud manner. Everyone in the bar froze, eyes on me, as if my actions could determine their future. And perhaps they could. I was tired of people underestimating me and mine.

Baz took a step back and even Mercy drew away, her movements taking her out of her chair and next to my cousin in the time it takes to blink. I pulled my glasses off and cleaned them with a handkerchief I found in my pocket. I replaced my glasses and folded the handkerchief carefully, tucking it back in my pocket.

"Consider yourself warned," I said. "You have threatened my family. You have insulted Baz, and therefore myself. I don't care what sort of power you have, if you attempt to harm Baz or anyone else connected with me, I will come at you with the full force of my ability."

Tiberius sneered and leaned back in his chair. "And what, you'll run a smear campaign on me? Ooooh, I'm so scared."

Iago and the others, whose names I hadn't bothered to learn, chuckled. I sighed, throwing every melodramatic instinct I had into the sound. "Death might have hired me to be his marketing agent, but I am so very much more than that."

Tiberius laughed, the sound low enough to mimic the bass in a car whose speaker systems were worth more than the engines. I resisted the urge to roll my eyes. "Very well, human. If you are so keen to challenge us, then give it your best shot. You—and your cousin—are now marked for Death, a bounty on your heads. We shall see how much your boss pays you when you are nothing more than a smear on the pavement."

"Good luck with that," I replied breezily, and turned from the table without a backwards glance. I gestured to Baz and Mercy, the two of them preceding me out the door. I closed it behind us with a little wave of my fingers then slammed the doorknob with the heel of my palm, snapping off the old metal and dropping it to the ground.

The bar shook with a roar of fury, which quieted to a simple click and vanished entirely. I brushed my hands together and nodded firmly at the door, turning back to my cousin and Mercy. Our ruse to get the giants to reveal their plan was torn to shreds, but I didn't really care. I would tear them apart with my bare hands if need be. Okay, maybe not my bare hands.

"Cal, how did you know that breaking the doorknob would sever the connection to the mortal realm?" Mercy asked, looking slightly impressed.

"Oh, I didn't. But I accidentally locked myself out of my flat once, and my friend Neja kicked in the doorknob. It opened just fine, but once I closed it from the other side, I couldn't get the thing open without calling a locksmith. I figured it would work sort of the same here," I said, kicking the doorknob with my shoe. "At least, the knob looks sort of like the one at my flat."

Mercy looked decidedly less impressed.

Baz leaped out of the shadows and tackled me, wrapping his arms around my middle and squeezing like his life depended on it. "Thank you, Cal," he whispered, voice wavering slightly. I patted him awkwardly on the back.

"I don't know why you're thanking him," Mercy grumbled, now scowling, arms folded. "He basically put a bounty on your head."

Baz straightened and slung his arm around my shoulder. "Yeah, but he did it because he cares about me!"

I sighed, removing Baz's arm by pinching his shirt sleeve and lifting it away from me. "Yes, well, that's nice and all, but I do think we should perhaps get off the street. I don't imagine the broken door will hold them for long."

Mercy rolled her eyes. "You severed the connection of the bar with the mortal realm. They will have to travel all the way back from Elsewhere, and it's not so easy to do when you are essentially a projection of a larger entity."

"I think we should have a conversation wherein you explain all of this stuff to me," I said. "And I think we should do it in a place where they serve proper coffee."

"I got Aunt Teresa a great coffee machine for her birthday last year," Baz said with a disturbing note of cheer in his step. "I can make you a cup at home. Anything for my best mate, Cal."

Before I could protest, Baz was already walking back towards my mother's house. I ran after him, Mercy on my heels. "I think I should be the one to use the coffee machine," I called. "Your coffee was terrible!"

"We are all going to die," Mercy grumbled, easily outpacing me and Baz both. "The balance is going to be destroyed and we are all going to die."

"Oh, please," I said. "I can't die."

"Yes, because that's so much comfort to me," Mercy snapped. It was possible she had a point.

6

HOME COOKING

When we returned to the house, my mother was there with a takeaway menu in hand, looking rather incongruous in her fancy clothes and purple house slippers with bunny ears on them. She took one look at the three of us and sighed.

"Should I bother to ask what you've done this time, Cal?" she asked, setting the menu and her phone on the counter.

"Why do you assume that I was the one who caused the problem?" I sidled towards the coffee machine. My mother fixed me with one of her signature stares, the sort that has everyone from the postal workers to the local politicians quaking in their boots. "Very well, I will admit that I neglected to pay my bar tab."

This earned me a glare and a frown, both of which were made worse when Baz cut in and said, "Oh, it's not a big deal. They'll just take it out of my last paycheque. If they bother to give me a last paycheque."

"You were fired?" my mother asked, an imperious arch to her brow.

Baz shrugged and put his hands into his pockets. "Well, I think I actually quit. By proxy. It's a little complicated."

"I see," she said, voice deadpan. Then, she looked at Mercy—immortal, preternaturally beautiful and deadly Mercy—and lifted the menu again. "Should I order food for all of us, or do you have other plans?"

I shrugged. "I mean, I don't know if—"

"Yes," Baz said firmly. "It's that great Indian place, right? The one with the naan soaked in honey and cinnamon and that rice pudding?"

"Yes," my mother said. "Well, I will order food. You three discuss whatever world-ending business you were planning on discussing."

"I'll make the coffee," I muttered, moving to the machine.

"Calvin Montgomery Thorpe!" My mother's voice rang across the room like a bell. A bell with barbed wire and an excess of bear traps. I winced and hunched my shoulders.

"Yes, Mother?"

"There will be no coffee this late in the evening. You know what it does to get so hyped up on caffeine before bed," she said. I looked longingly at the coffee machine, but sat in a chair at the table instead.

"Yes, Mother."

I knew coming home was a bad idea.

With that, my mother picked up her phone and took it, and the menu, to another room. As soon as she had gone, Mercy collapsed in a chair and started laughing, the sound enough to add insult to injury. I hunched my shoulders further.

"It's not funny," I grumbled. Mercy wiped a tear from her eye.

"Oh, trust me, it's *hilarious*. I understand so much about you, now. I mean, really, everything about you makes so much sense!" Mercy laid her head on the table and kept laughing, the sound muffled by a curtain of her hair, but still clear enough.

I muttered something impolite and folded my arms, sinking into the chair. Baz patted my shoulder and sat on my other side. "Don't worry, Cal. I like you and Aunt Teresa just fine."

That really didn't help. I decided to keep my mouth shut and change the topic very quickly. I didn't need Mercy thinking any worse of me than she already did. Though, I supposed that the giggles was far better than abject loathing. Not to mention that even if she hated me, she wouldn't let it get in the way of doing her duty. Still, it was hardly encouraging.

"So, can you explain to me *now* what is going on?" I asked, putting as much ire as I could muster into the question. "I mean, what's with the whole giant-not-giant thing? And just what sort of situation do I have to fix? I mean, I got Baz out of there, so he's not under their control anymore, but I doubt that I was sent here for that. No offense, Baz."

"None taken," he said, still smiling. "I'm just glad you're home, even if the potential apocalypse was the reason."

"Surely it's not *that* bad," I muttered. "I mean, Life indicated that it was more an inconvenience than anything, not that I really trust Life at all."

Mercy gathered her composure as if it had never left, once more the stoic, proper assassin sitting at my table. She studied Baz for a moment, then me, and a hard glint entered her eye. "Since you are both obviously ignorant of the ways of the world, I will enlighten you. The mortal realm was separated from Elsewhere back before anyone can remember."

"Yeah, I know this," I said. "Some guy named Carteria managed to separate the realms and his residual power was placed into a stupid amulet that somehow can't seem to stay where it is put no matter how many times I lock it away and, ah, that is... I'm familiar with the story."

Mercy glared at me, and if looks could kill I would be dead several times over. She lifted her chin. "As I was saying, the mortal realm was separated from Elsewhere. The majority of the magic went to Elsewhere and the beings that reside there, with certain provisions put into place for crossing the boundaries. Many of the beings who remained in the mortal realms lost their connection with their source magic and, therefore, lost their immortality and a great deal of power.

They became more on par with humans, the dominant species of the mortal realm."

"Cool!" Baz said. "So there are magical beings running around that are like us?"

Mercy rolled her eyes. I frowned. "Well, those that I've met are certainly closer to mortals—er, humans—than many of their Elsewhere counterparts." I had met more than a few Fae on both sides, and the ones on the Elsewhere side were certainly more volatile, more dangerous. Vampires were problematic no matter where I met them.

So far, I was following what Mercy was saying. I mean, I had no idea what the separation of the mortal realms from Elsewhere had to do with a bunch of people trying to kill my family, but I was following. Mostly. There were still a lot of unanswered questions.

Mercy held up a hand to forestall me; I snapped my mouth closed and waited for her to continue. "It's incredibly complicated, but the simple version is that both Elsewhere and the mortal realms still require magic to function. Therefore, some beings were left here to provide a type of source magic and allow the beings of a more magical nature to survive. This magic required management, but it was deemed too unstable to leave to one entity or species. Like Life and Death, it requires balance to function, to continue."

I had the distinct feeling that Mercy was dumbing down her explanation of the theoretical magical principles to the level of maybe a trained beagle so that I could understand. I had lived in Elsewhere for a goodly amount of time, but theoretical magic was way, way beyond me. I preferred marketing. Thankfully, Baz looked even more confused than I felt, his mouth hanging open and his eyebrows straining for his hairline. Still, I didn't need a thorough understanding of magical physics to figure out what was going on with the giants and the potential end of the world.

"Okay," I said slowly, drawing out the word so I could think. "The giants are one side of the balance to keep the magical source going, right?"

Mercy nodded. "Correct. They rule Beneath."

"Beneath the ground?" Baz interrupted. He looked a little worried, or perhaps he was just ill.

"Just Beneath. It is more a metaphorical concept than a literal one," Mercy said. I winced; metaphor and magic had gotten me into a great deal of trouble more than once. Without my soul, I operated far closer to logic than emotion and metaphor made no sense at all.

"And Above?" I asked, not entirely sure I wanted to know the answer.

"The rulers of Above are what you humans call exousia," Mercy said, as though that explained everything. I looked to Baz to see if he understood what she was talking about. He shrugged and shook his head.

Mercy groaned, a sound I was quite familiar with. "Do you know nothing? What do they *teach* humans these days? Exousia are—"

"Exousia are a class of angels known as Authorities. They are the fifth class of angels, responsible for maintaining balance and order in the universe." My mother stood in the doorway to the kitchen, looking perfectly calm, phone in hand. But she wasn't reading from her phone; the screen was blank and she was staring directly at the three of us.

"Exactly!" Mercy said. "Thank you."

I held up my hand. "First, angels are real? What am I saying, of course they're real. Vampires are real. Were-wolves, rock trolls, all of that is real. Why not angels? Second, how do you know about that, Mum?"

My mother rolled her eyes, a huge display of feeling from her. She minced across the kitchen, still wearing her bunny slippers, and sank gracefully into a chair across from me. Mercy looked as though she approved. "I have been going to church my entire life, Cal. Not to mention, I do have access to these things called books. Strange pieces of paper with ink on them, occasionally bound in leather, though modern ones are bound in cloth or cardboard."

Well, apparently I was in for a treat if my mother was in a sarcastic mood. Normally she preferred to be simply stoic and calm, but I will acknowledge that I learned my sarcasm from her. I was nowhere near her level of mastery.

"Wow, Aunt Teresa," Baz said, clearly in awe. "So, there are more different sorts of angels?"

My mother opened her mouth to say something, but Mercy held up her hand. "If I may, I don't wish to interrupt, but I must cut this short. We are not possessed of an abundance of time."

"Of course," my mother said, inclining her head

like royalty. She obeyed Mercy's request without argument or hesitation. My goodness, could the evening get stranger?

Mercy nodded. "In short, angels of all classes are the messengers to the gods, the Elderkin if you will. Many of them no longer interact with the humans, or they've been forgotten and have faded from existence, but their messengers remain. The Judaic, Christian, and Islamic tradition of angels are the most common. Exousia are the ones meant to maintain the working order of things and were therefore chosen as rulers of Above."

I nodded, twice. This was all a bit surreal, even in my detached state. I was feeling a little out of my depth, frankly. Most of my jobs for Death had been relatively small in scope: solve a murder, do some relationship counselling, get someone to pay back taxes, watch Death's pets for a couple of days. Okay, I will freely admit that on more than one occasion, events had turned into potentially really bad situations, with the fate of Elsewhere at stake. But they always started out small. Now, I was barely into my first day back home and I was already dealing with giants and angels and apocalypses. Or, well, potential apocalypses. I didn't actually know precisely what was going on, after all. Mercy hadn't gotten that far in her lecture.

I really needed some coffee.

My mother must have caught my longing look at the shiny chrome-and-black machine on the counter, because she shook her head firmly. "Coffee tomorrow,

Cal. The food will be here in twenty minutes, surely you can just wait until then."

I lowered my head to the table and tried to swallow back a groan. "Did you know that I was given *vacation time* to sort this out? It was just supposed to be a simple matter of getting Baz to stop dealing Dragonwort—"

I lifted my head at Baz and glared. "You *have* stopped dealing Dragonwort, right?"

Baz chuckled, the sort of sound that one usually makes right before an admission of guilt. "Well, I mean, yeah. I haven't dealt in that stuff for maybe a couple of months, now?"

I lowered my head to the table again. "Okay, Mercy, lay it on me. Life and Death said that the balance of the mortal realm was in danger, that they couldn't allow so great a shift to happen. So, what, are the giants and Exousia going to war? Is that what this is about? Do I have to stop a war, again?"

Silence met my words and I waited a beat, thinking that maybe it was just that Mercy was calculating her words, doing her best to figure out how to explain to a stupid human what was going on. The silence continued. I lifted my head and found her staring at me, mouth open, as if she could not possibly believe my inability to do anything at all, let alone be the one sent to sort this out.

"What?" I demanded. My mother looked pointedly at her phone, the screen flashing like she was sorting through her photographs. Baz twiddled his thumbs.

Like actually, literally, twiddled his thumbs. He looked fervently at the table.

"Cal...if one side or the other gets complete control, it would be bad."

"Yes, I *understand* that," I said, "but what does it mean? Life and Death indicated that it would be some sort of apocalypse situation. Maybe. They didn't actually give me any specifics. They did imply that, I don't know, the world would end? It was all tied to Baz dealing Dragonwort."

Mercy snorted. "As if one human dealing a tiny amount of Dragonwort could affect the balance."

Baz glared at the table. "It's not my fault."

"No, it's not, and be glad that you are too insignificant to change things." Mercy was edging dangerously close to a sneer. My mother pinched her lips together and her nostrils flared. I understood the sentiment exactly.

"Baz is not insignificant," I said. Baz flashed me a grateful smile.

"I did not say it was a bad thing," Mercy retorted. This was about to turn into one of those really bad arguments that destroy kitchen furniture; the only question was whether I would start the fight or my mother would. I'd give even odds for my mother and Mercy.

"Continue your explanation," my mother said, voice frigid. Baz shivered. Mercy inhaled sharply, but nodded.

"Let me see if I can explain this simply for you,"

Mercy said. "Can things that are above become beneath?"

"What, like sky versus earth sort of a thing? Above the ground versus Beneath the ground?" I felt like I was getting a lesson in language and semantics. While I usually thought of myself as a pretty capable guy when it came to language and communication, this was a bit ridiculous.

"Yes," Mercy said.

"Well, no. I mean, things that are above the ground cannot be under the ground unless they're dead. Like Life and Death cannot take each other's place, no matter how much they try." I was beginning to get a grasp of what was going on, and I didn't much like it.

"Exactly. Think of them the same way. The Dragonwort is just a small symptom, a visible sign that the giants are rallying their allies, trying to make them stronger, more numerous. The exousia will react to this, possibly providing their allies with a better means to fight against the augmented powers of Beneath. They won't actually go after each other, because they can't." Mercy looked at me, as if waiting for me to fill in the gaps.

I groaned. Understanding began to dawn on me, and it was more of a bother than anything. This wasn't about some world-ending apocalypse after all. The giants and exousia couldn't go after each other any more than Life and Death could go after each other. Though, I had once gotten in the middle of Life and Death while they were having an argument and had been literally disintegrated. I got better, though, and sorted things out.

Somehow, I doubted either the giants or exousia would be satisfied with beating each other up until they each walked away bruised and bloody. No, they were going to send their allies to war.

"We're going to have to sort out a whole bunch of itty bitty arguments that are really a proxy for the giants and exousia," I said, hoping I was wrong. Maybe an apocalypse would be easier. "We have to keep the magical community from tearing itself into pieces, because the humans would notice that, and that would be bad."

Baz shrugged, drawing his fingers over the grain of wood in the table. "I mean, would it really be that bad? Aunt Teresa and I are aware of the magical world, and we're not...well, you know, freaking out."

"Speak for yourself, Basil," my mother said with a sniff. "Do you have any idea how hard it is not to tell my friends about my current houseguest, who is supposed to be dead? I mean, my goodness, if I buy one extra thing at the shops, they'll assume that I've either got a boyfriend, or something very strange is going on."

"I'll try not to be seen by anyone we know," I said, doing my best to reassure my mother. Of course, that would be easier said than done. My mother was friends with a huge number of people around the city, and at one point, I hadn't been able to walk to work without being stopped by someone she knew.

"Of course it would be bad!" Mercy snapped, completely ignoring our discussion of shops and acquaintances. The three of us looked apologetically at her; none of us were terribly good at staying on topic. "Every news station and paper and internet site would be full of panic. There would be whole communities killed. The world would *collapse* into chaos."

I tapped my mouth, thinking. "So, every conspiracy theory nut would be proved right, all in a matter of a very short amount of time."

"Oh," Baz said. "I guess that would be bad."

"Right," I agreed. "Well, then, Mercy. What are we going to do about it?"

Mercy looked as though she were about to beat me into a very small pulp, like she wanted to tear off my head and feed it to Death's dogs, Mischief and Mayhem. I seemed to have this effect on her, and had done since our first meeting. Granted, it had gotten a little worse after I rescued Agravane from the clutches of her Order of Silence, and it was discovered I couldn't die. I decided to wait until she had finished her deep breathing exercise before pressing her for answers.

"We must stop the distribution of Dragonwort and other magical weapons by the giants, for one," Mercy said, holding up a finger. "That will reduce the need for the allies of Above to directly oppose the allies of Below. It won't stop the petty fighting, but it will help keep the conflicts manageable."

"Okay, stop a drug and weapons trade," I said. "What else?"

Mercy held up another finger. "We need to put the giants back in their prison, so they can't directly communicate with their allies. They will have to go back to simply existing, like the exousia, and neither side will provoke the other."

I blinked. Sat back in my chair. Fiddled with my phone. Coughed once. "Seriously? That's *it?*"

"These are giants, Cal," Mercy snarled. "They are awake enough that they can manifest physical forms to walk the earth. They will not go back to prison easily."

I threw up my hands, the full force of an overdramatic emotional frustration hitting me right in the head. All my pent up or ignored emotion seemed to rise to the surface, and suddenly it was impossible to exert any control, to act at all logical. "Stop some drug trade and put a few giants in prison. I mean, *seriously,* you were acting like this is way, way, beyond anything I've ever done in the past. My goodness, Mercy, it's difficult, but not impossible. When will people stop underestimating me!"

Mercy glared at me with all the power at her disposal. "I cannot determine if you are simply ignorant, or if it is a universal human arrogance. You understand *nothing* of the way of the world."

I opened my mouth to argue that I was doing just fine with the ways of the world, that it was the world which was broken. I felt Sebastian writhing itself awake inside me and the world took on a slightly yellow tinge, a sign that my Reaper abilities were active.

"Calvin," my mother snapped. I closed my mouth with a click and settled back into the chair. Sebastian grumbled but was not dumb enough to disobey my mother.

"All I'm saying is that this is not the most complicated job I've had," I muttered. "It's still way, way outside my contract of *marketing agent*, but perfectly manageable."

Mercy looked as though she wanted to argue—possibly with actual physical blows—but the doorbell rang. Baz leaped from his chair. "Food's here!"

He dashed off to the door and my mother rolled her eyes. "Always the peacemaker, that one. No impulse control at all. Terrible combination."

I was going to argue, since Baz wasn't *that* bad, but we heard a scuffling sound and a terrified scream. "You are *not* the food delivery person!"

I sighed and went to go help my cousin. Looks like the job couldn't even wait until after dinner to get complicated. It occurred to me that I might have spoken too soon, but surely Life wouldn't be *that* cruel.

Right?

HOME IS WHERE THE HEART IS

I found Baz lying on his back, his arms held up and out to deflect the slavering monster that was trying to close its jaws around his neck. It didn't look much like a shapeshifter, but nor did it look like a gremlin or a goblin or anything so well-defined. It looked, mostly, like someone had taken a shark and bred it with a dog, then added a snake's tail and massive yellow paws.

"Bad doggie!" Baz screamed, the creature getting closer with every snap of its jaws. The reprimand didn't seem to deter the thing at all, so I ran forwards and kicked its side. The thing pulled back from Baz, who immediately scooted away, and growled at me, a low rumbling deep in its chest.

"Try it," I said, holding out my hands like I had some idea of how to defend myself. Agravane had told me that my "game face" was generally passable, enough to deter things that were not violence prone anyways. Of course, I had then asked why I would need to defend myself against things that weren't violence prone, and received a sound thrashing as a result. We gave up on self-defence lessons soon thereafter.

The creature leaped for me, claws outstretched, jaws snapping for my face. I managed a single blow to the thing's chest, but that didn't deter it much. It latched onto my left shoulder and started shaking, like an alligator or a dog with a new toy. I nearly fainted.

Sebastian, on the other hand, woke up with a vengeance.

People—namely Agravane and Neja—made fun of me for naming my Reaper abilities, as if it was a separate entity and had a mind of its own. There was a reason for my choice, though, and it was because it *did* have a mind of its own. A goodly portion of the time, we acted in accord, the powers surging when I managed to actually feel emotion, or when I called it up. The rest of the time, Sebastian did things like take over my body and rain destruction down on the world.

Or, well, so I assumed, because this was the first time it had taken over in quite so dramatic a fashion.

My vision turned greyscale, except for bright yellow-gold auras surrounding all the living things in my vicinity. I could tell that the trembling yellow came from Baz, whose heart was pumping nothing but adrenaline through him. The steadier yet muted yellow came from my mother, who was calmer and still closer to Death simply by virtue of her age.

Mercy was almost a pure gold, tinged with silver, the touch of an immortal who was slightly beyond my capabilities. The thing latched onto my shoulder, though, was furious neon, writhing with rage and purpose.

I brought up my right hand and touched it, separating the neon yellow from the body. The creature let out a shriek of horror and let go of me, eyes darting in all directions, seeming to move in slow motion as gravity took hold and it fell, paws flailing. It was dead before it hit the ground.

The power of the thing's lifeforce flowed through me, settling into my inner being, the core of where Sebastian lived, like a drug. For a brief moment, I felt things like a normal person did. Fear, pain, even elation at having defeated my enemy. It was invigorating, intoxicating, and so *close* to what it felt like to have a soul that I immediately wanted more. Then, it vanished, the creature hardly strong enough to sustain the high for more than a heartbeat.

Sebastian roared in disappointment and retreated to go nurse the memory of that power, leaving me on my knees, hand pressed to my wounded shoulder, panting. The colour returned to my vision and I tentatively lifted my hand, looking to see how much blood there was.

It was a nonfatal injury, so it wouldn't heal until the next time I died—or if, for a change, I actually managed to heal on my own—but it hurt like the blazes. "Well, piffle," I said, forcing my lungs to stop heaving and take normal, controlled breaths. "I liked that suit."

My words seemed to be a key or a trigger or something, because the world started moving in what felt like double time. Baz was shouting something incoherent, still scrambling backwards. My mother was at his side, her arm around his shoulder and her expression more fierce than I'd ever seen it before. She flicked her gaze between me and the body of the creature, and the fierceness morphed into fear, her eyes wide and pupils dilated. Mercy stepped between me and my family, her own expression one of pure shock.

"Cal..." Mercy breathed, and I noted for the first time that there was a knife in her hand, the blade shining silver and pointed not at the dead thing, but at me. "What *was* that?"

"Oh, that?" I debated struggling to my feet, but decided that I should perhaps stay where I was. I wouldn't want to fall over and get more blood everywhere. "I have no idea. I mean, I've never seen anything like it. And I don't know of any stories that describe similar beings, so...I could take a picture and send it to Yolanda, see if she knows."

Mercy shook her head. "Not the chimera. What you did."

I shrugged, then winced, my shoulder protesting that course of action greatly. "Ow. Okay that hurts," I grumbled. Then, looking at Mercy, I said in a clearer voice, "That was Sebastian. My Reaper abilities."

Mercy swore. Loudly. In several languages, most of

which I didn't recognise. "The thing earlier and... and...*that* were a magnitude of scale different from each other."

"Well, Sebastian was asleep, earlier," I pointed out. I mean, really, shouldn't an assassin with the Order of Silence, dedicated to balance, know these things? "Though," I admitted, "it's usually not so loud. More precise, rather than bang, wham, dead sort of thing."

"That thing..." my mother rasped. She licked her lips and cleared her throat. "That thing was you?"

"Yes," I said. "Of course it was, couldn't you tell?"

Mercy shook her head. "No, Cal, it didn't look like you at all. One minute, the chimera was attacking you, and the next, it was like Death himself had appeared, a void ready to devour everything in its path, and then some. And what you did...it shouldn't be possible, whatever it is."

I huffed slightly. "I don't see why everyone is so upset. I explained my Reaper abilities, and it's all perfectly under control. I mean, shouldn't we be more concerned with this...this...thing that attacked us? Or, well, attacked you, Baz."

Baz was still looking a bit shaken, his face pale and his hair sticking up at odd angles where he had dragged it against the floor. My mother stood up, tugging at her dress to straighten it out. Baz stood also, the two of them almost leaning on each other for support. It was nice to see that they had developed such a strong bond since I'd been gone, but it was a little strange. I'd never had that sort of relationship with my mother, nor had she with anyone else that I knew. Perhaps I'd never needed one. Perhaps she hadn't, either.

Mercy walked over to the dead creature and poked it with her shoe. She shrugged. "It's a chimera. A sort of conglomeration, beings made entirely of magic, drawing on the traits of one or more animals. From the original Greek Chimera. They are pests, and decent hunters, but hardly worth your reaction."

This last was said with a firm glare.

"It bit me," I complained. I lifted my hand to show the evidence, then pressed it back down, my shoulder complaining. "It was instinct."

"You need to hone your instincts," Mercy hissed, her voice low. She flicked her eyes to where my family stood, watching. "People might die if you do not."

My rational brain told me that there was something I was missing. This all seemed like an overreaction to Sebastian to me, but I wasn't going to waste time arguing with them to defend myself. I could not change what I was, nor what I'd done. Nor did I think that a conversation about Death and inevitability was going to help the situation. As far as I could tell, the best course of action would be to keep moving forwards. The others could adapt—or not—as they saw fit. I knew that it should bother me more than it did, but there was nothing I could do, to either help them or make myself be bothered by their reaction.

One of the things that is essential to marketing is that you cannot force someone into making a decision.

You have to be subtle, prod them gently, or the more you push, the more they'll resist. It was sometimes the hardest thing to do. But enough saturation and enough exposure and people will eventually come to accept something. Eventually.

"Okay," I said. "So, what, the giants sent this thing after Baz?"

Mercy studied me for a moment, then helped me to my feet. She led me to the kitchen and practically pushed me into the chair. My mother and Baz followed, keeping a bit more space between them and me. Mercy started poking through cabinets until she found some towels and a first aid kit. "Possible. Though, I think that was more a bounty hunter's attempt. Not all of them are so powerful, and they will often rely on such creatures when dealing with easy prey, such as a single human."

"I'm not sure whether I should be offended by that or not," Baz said. He sounded less shaky than he looked, which was a good sign. He took the first aid kit from Mercy and started tending to my shoulder, being less gentle with my ruined suit as he could have been. I decided not to protest. It was unlikely that my mother would let me wander around the streets of London in a ruined suit, in any case.

That is, if she would actually look at me again. At the moment, she was leaning against a wall, her phone clutched tightly in her hands. "Dinner will be here in about five minutes," she murmured into the silence.

"Like I said," Mercy continued, throwing away the

ruined towels, "the giants are going to have a while before they can return to this realm in any sort of capable form. Travel between realms is not as easy for most as it is for Life and Death."

"That's good, right?" Baz asked, pressing an antibiotic to my shoulder. I wondered if I was meant to register the stinging as pain or just an annoyance.

"In general, yes," Mercy said. "It will give us more time to prepare for their return. We need to at least destroy the Dragonwort supply, and whatever other weapons they've stockpiled before they can reform. Then we can determine how to imprison them, without interference from their allies."

Baz nodded, putting a gauze pad on my shoulder. He taped it down with rather less efficiency than I would like, but I was willing to forgive him, given the circumstances. Besides, I'd had worse medical care, and it wasn't like it would kill me. It definitely hurt, though.

"Yeah, I can take you to some of the people who helped with the distribution tomorrow. I mean, I don't know where the warehouse is, exactly, but I'm sure we can figure it out." Baz gave a weak smile.

It would have to be good enough. Mercy nodded, and my mother held up her phone to indicate that the food was there. For the rest of the evening, I did my best to play perfect guest, helping to serve up the food and keeping the conversation flowing by asking Baz and my mother all sorts of questions about things that had changed while I'd been gone. I even relayed some of the more harmless antics performed by Yolanda and Agravane, such as their fondness for soap operas and an inability to understand human things like electricity bills and how to drive an automobile.

It was a terribly awkward evening. Despite the stories and the muted laughter, I could feel them staring at me every few minutes. Mercy focused on Baz and my mother rather than on me, and ate her food with politeness, though she turned her nose up at the curry. The others tried to keep me in the conversation, but it was like an invisible barrier had been put up. I couldn't tell whether it was because I had died—well, mostly died—and come back, or if it was because of the earlier incident with Sebastian.

I guess it's true what they say: you can't go home again.

Especially not after Death removed you from the fate of the world.

With a tentative plan in place to go find Baz's distribution acquaintances the next morning, eventually we all wandered up to bed. I was given a place to sleep on the couch, since Baz now slept in what had been my bedroom growing up. Thankfully, none of my stuff from my previous life had been there except a few pictures and a well-deflated football from my one attempt to join a sports team in school. My flat had been in a different part of the city, and I had been allowed to bring a good portion of my things to Elsewhere. So it wasn't strange, per se, that Baz slept in my old room. But it was certainly unusual to be relegated to the couch in my childhood home, since Mercy was given the guest room.

I wore a pair of borrowed pyjama pants from Baz, featuring tiny spaceships, and tried not to rub my injured shoulder too hard. The couch was also new, a leather piece that fit the decor of the house much better than the chintz sofa from my youth. It was a little short for me, my toes hanging over the edge of one of the arms. I turned over, trying to get into a more comfortable position. Someone was standing in the doorway to the living room, wrapped in a dressing gown and bunny slippers.

"Hello, Mum," I said, sitting up. My mother glided into the room.

"Cal, I have to ask," she said, folding her arms around herself. "Was it...did you really have to leave two years ago? Was there another way?"

I shrugged. "I was shot, Mum. The only reason I'm still alive now is because Death came to hire me at the only time he could. The Instant of Death. It's not like I could have just refused him and kept on living my life. Trust me, I asked."

My mother frowned. "It's just...things have not been easy since you left. Despite appearances. I don't speak to your father's half of the family at all, since they thought that I didn't deserve your insurance money, amongst other difficult conversations."

I winced a little at that. My father had died when I was young and things had always been a little weird between my mother and that half of the family, despite them being Thorpes and claiming me as part of their lineage. I wasn't surprised that things had gotten more complicated since my leaving.

"And Baz," my mother continued, ignoring my reaction. "He lost his best friend, Cal. He couldn't hold down a job properly, not until this last one, and he was basically disowned because he wasn't living up to the standards placed upon him as a Thorpe. I just want you to know what it was like, so that you understand."

I thought she probably wanted a little more than that, but with my emotions all haywire after the situation with Sebastian, I wasn't sure I could do more than understand. I nodded. "Trust me, I wouldn't have left if there had been a better option."

"But what about when you're done this time? Will you just leave again without a second glance? Will you even be able to call?"

Ah. *Now* I understood. She didn't want me to just disappear again, upsetting their lives for a short time and then waltzing off into the sunset because I was some sort of important person in Elsewhere. Not that I wasn't replaceable, just that I was in a unique situation.

"I doubt Death and Life would have sent me back here otherwise. I may not be able to visit much, but I have a feeling that they'll let me call or text or email or whatever. Otherwise, they could have just as easily sent only Mercy, or someone else, and solved the problem that way." I hoped I was right, because the alternative would be problematic.

My mother nodded. "Very well. But I should warn

you, it will not be easy on Baz when you do leave, even if you call."

"I'll see what I can do," I said. With that, she turned around and left, not a second glance or a backwards look. At least some things were the same. I lay back on the couch and tried to cover my toes with the blanket. Then, I fell into a fitful sleep, wherein I dreamed about werewolves and Mercy trying to kill me, and Yolanda renting a whole lot of movies to fill the time while Agravane tried to put out a fire in the office.

8

HOME SWEET HOME

The next morning, I was awoken by a sharp poke to the ribs, which was likely meant to get me fully awake in a very short amount of time. Unfortunately, I had been well acclimated to such efforts. Agravane found them very entertaining, and the few times Neja stopped by before I was awake and caffeinated, she liked to see just what sort of reaction she could cause by prodding me in the internal organs.

Of course, I also often went without sleep, since my soulless state meant that I was not entirely bound by such physical needs as food and sleep. Death had once explained it as a residual effect of my relative immortality—something about my lifeforce replacing my soul or some such nonsense—taking over where my strictly physical reactions would be. It had involved a decent amount of biology and chemistry and I got distracted halfway through the conversation because Death's necktie was crooked.

Actually, a fair number of relatively important conversations had a similar outcome since my soul had vanished. I was apt to focus on tiny details rather than the big picture. Not that I had been terribly good at big picture thinking before the loss of my soul, but the effect had definitely gotten worse.

I pulled the blanket over my shoulder and rolled over, grumbling at whoever it was to go away. In return, I had the blanket snatched away completely and was hit with a wave of slightly frigid air.

I rolled back over on the couch and cracked open an eye. I was met with a blurry image of what I thought was Mercy, since she was the only woman in the house who was likely to walk around in full medieval-style dress, a belt with a dagger on her hip. I felt around the coffee table for my glasses, then instinctively checked the time on my phone.

"Seriously?" I asked. "It's five in the morning. Why are you waking me up at five in the morning? Is the house on fire?"

Mercy frowned. "Why is your first assumption that the house is on fire? Would it not be more conceivable that I simply wanted to get an early start?"

I sat up and stretched. Swallowed once to get rid of the strange taste in my mouth. "I would think it more or less irrelevant what time we got started, as it were. Baz is the one who has to introduce us to his associates, and there is little guarantee that they would even be awake this early. Now, if it were nighttime, I might agree with you; I have found that most unsavoury characters prefer to do business late at night as opposed to early in the morning. But would they get up early, when the cafes and bakeries open and people are running around for exercise, and there are no bars or restaurants or banks open? No. It is much better to sleep in, to do business when most people are awake and—"

Mercy put a hand over my mouth. "Stop. Talking."

I blinked. Had I been talking? "I haven't had any coffee, yet. My brain is only functioning part of the way."

"Considering I have yet to see your brain functioning at full capacity no matter what time of day, that is a ridiculous argument. However, Baz is not yet awake, and you require a shower and a change of your bandages. Chimeras are not generally venomous, but they do carry rather a lot of bacteria in their saliva."

That thought struck me as potentially significant. I looked down at the bandages peeking our from beneath my t-shirt. "Fine," I said, and went to go take a shower. "Please can you at least have some coffee ready for me when I am done?"

I didn't wait for Mercy to agree or decline, just trudged off. She was right, despite waking me before the sun was even up. A shower made everything feel much better, and cleaning the wounds lifted some of the residual discomfort that was likely due to the start of an infection. By the time I made it down the stairs, wearing a fresh t-shirt and my trousers from the day before, I felt almost normal.

Well, whatever my normal was.

Also when I emerged, the table was being set for breakfast. My mother was up and dressed in a vintage style pantsuit, straight out of the forties, and Baz was hunched at the table in a dressing gown I recognised as once having been mine. He looked even more bleary-eyed than usual, and had a cup of coffee clutched in his hands.

I immediately went and prepared my own coffee, sniffing deeply before taking a tentative sip. I winced. "Did you make this, Baz?"

"Good morning to you, too, Cal. No, I'm feeling much better after being almost eaten alive last night, thanks for asking. My mental state will be perfectly fine." Baz took a bite of some toast and muttered more of the same under his breath.

"One of these days, I will teach you how to make proper coffee," I informed him. He stuck his tongue out at me.

"It's like having teenagers in the house all over again," my mother said with a definitive sigh. "Am I going to have to separate you two?"

Baz and I shook our heads. I made some toast and sat at the table, staring at the coffee. Mercy joined us, her expression just as grave as it had been the night before. It was going to be one of those days, then.

"I'm going to work," my mother announced, though I doubted that her shift at the local library started before seven in the morning. Without a backwards glance, she strode away and left the three of us to our scheming. Or, rather, left us so Baz could grouse at me some more.

"I haven't seen her like this since your funeral," Baz said. "It really messed her up, Cal. You should be more careful."

"I was not really given a choice in the manner of my disappearance. I cannot undo what Death did, nor would he care." I fixed Baz with a look, wondering if the face he made was considered rude, or if he just wasn't properly awake, yet. Without similar emotional abilities, I was not very good at interpreting others' expressions.

"Yeah, but you just *left*, Cal. We thought you were *dead*. Do you even realise what that means? What that was like?" Baz stared into his mug, and even I could figure out what that meant. I was having the same conversation with Baz that I'd had with my mother; this was a very strange experience.

"You are welcome to blame me all you like, Baz, but I truly had no choice. It was either this or actual death. And before you yell at me for not calling after I was established, remember that Death removed me from the fate of the world. The *entire* world." I stared at Baz until he looked away again. His shoulders sagged and he looked even more miserable than he had after the chimera attack.

Mercy sighed. "I say this because it is my nature to be merciful. Removing Cal from the fate of the world was no small feat. You are fortunate that you are able to interact with him normally right now. Any other person besides yourself and Teresa will not be able to process the interaction. They know Cal to be dead, and they will continue to see Cal as dead. Do not underestimate the reality of the situation just because he is here with you, now."

Baz blinked at Mercy, then at me. "So, what, you're saying I'll forget Cal is alive after all this is done?"

"No. You will be aware of his existence, but no one else will believe you. And this Cal is not the same one who left," Mercy said, her voice surprisingly gentle. She had never spoken to me like that, though that wasn't a great shock to me. She did loathe me, after all. "You expect the same things of Cal now as you did then. Do not do so. You will only be set up for disappointment."

Baz looked at me for a long moment, staring long past what was generally considered to be polite. He seemed to be studying every inch of me, from my glasses to the bandages on my shoulder, watching my face for something, then looking at the rest of me as if I had suddenly changed into some sort of alien.

"Yeah," Baz said after a minute. "Okay."

Without precisely knowing why, I deflated a bit.

We ate in silence for a while. Part of me wondered if I was meant to be bothered by what had just happened, but I decided it was irrelevant. I had a job to do, and would figure out the emotional and social ramifications of the situation once I had a chance to talk it over with someone who could still feel things properly. Or when I had an episode where the emotions filtered through whatever veil was between me and them. Though, those usually ended badly.

"So, um, should we get to finding my associates?" Baz asked after he had pushed his empty mug away. Mercy nodded and Baz fled before I could add my thoughts to the situation.

"How strange," I said. "He's not normally so flighty."

"Normal things just pass you by, don't they, Cal?" Mercy asked, finishing off the last of her coffee.

"Well, I suppose. Though that could do with the fact that I am often caught up in very abnormal circumstances. I believe it is a consequence of working for Death. I do have my suspicions that Life likes to throw obstacles my direction just to see how I will react, however. She is that sort."

Mercy shook her head. "Keep telling yourself that."

I shrugged and decided it would be easier not to argue with Mercy. She had known Life and Death for longer than I, but my interactions with them had been of a more unusual nature. At least, I hoped that was the case; if they interacted with everyone the way they did me, then there was something more fundamentally wrong with the universe than I had anticipated.

Baz returned a few minutes later, freshly showered and wearing clothes that at least appeared clean. He had exchanged his Tiny Dinosaurs With Phasers shirt for a Beatles shirt and had an umbrella in hand. "Right," he said with a wide smile. "Shall we sort this out?"

London has this annoying propensity for drizzle. Sometimes, it turns into proper rain, but most of the time, it just drizzles. Endlessly. Baz's umbrella turned out to be an omen for the day, and we spent several miserable episodes trudging from bus stop to bus stop, going through quiet streets and eventually ending up in a part of the city where industrial estates and warehouses were more common than coffee shops and Nando's.

Finally, we stopped at a tiny fish and chips shop that was tucked between a Tesco and a wholesale butcher, meant to serve the workers for the local print shop and some clothing manufacturers. It was, understandably for the middle of the morning during the week, empty except for the restaurant worker who was leaning on the counter with his attention diverted into his phone. He did not even look up when we entered.

I took a deep breath, the smell of fried fish and malt vinegar as familiar as my childhood home. It was a smell exclusive to the cheapest fish and chips shops and promised exquisite food that was really, really terrible for you. It was the smell of London, and I liked it. A lot. I went up to the counter.

"Cal!" Mercy snapped. "What are you doing?"

"I want a standard fish and chip meal," I said, handing over some coins I had scrounged from my mother's purse. I would pay her back. Eventually. The man at the counter looked up and yawned.

"Yeah, okay," he said, taking the money and heading back to the warming dishes, where he served up a heaping portion of chips and a slab of fish. I took the food and poured vinegar over it, finally turning to join my companions at their tiny plastic table.

"We don't have time for food," Mercy said, reaching out to take my meal away from me. I cradled the container close to me.

"I wanted fish and chips," I said. "I haven't had them for years, okay?"

"Actually, we might be here for a bit," Baz said, plucking a chip from my basket. He stuffed it into his mouth and continued talking. "The people we're looking for aren't usually around until lunch."

"Who, exactly, are we looking for?" Mercy asked, sniffing in disdain when I offered her a chip. "And I can't believe you would eat that crap. It is beyond unhealthy."

"But it tastes good," I said. Baz nodded agreement.

"It's the best I've ever had, and I've had a fair amount. Anyways, we want two people, a Maxine and a Thomas. Maxine is tiny, like a dancer but faster. You'll recognise her by her hair; it's usually purple. Or green. And then Thomas—"

"Let me guess," Mercy said drily, "Thomas is a demon." She nodded her head to two people who were approaching the shop, their expressions slightly obscured by the dirty window. The smaller one had vibrant purple hair in a standard pixie cut, her movements precise and flowing and probably very, very dangerous. The other was nearing seven feet in height, his clothes appropriate for the set of a movie about

1930s gangsters, complete with hat and jacket. He had a beard that would make an American redneck proud and I'm fairly certain that there were horns poking through the brim of his fedora.

"Wow, like an actual demon?" I asked. I mean, considering there were actual angels, I shouldn't have been surprised that demons were around, but I hadn't really considered the implications. "Is he going to try and corrupt my soul?"

"You don't have a soul to corrupt, and we are not talking about demons from hell. That's a different sort entirely," Mercy said with a very clear rolling of her eyes. "A demon as in scion of vampire and a mortal witch. They're relatively capable, as far as magical beings go, but they rely more on intelligence than physical force."

Baz chuckled, watching Thomas approach. "I wouldn't say Thomas is quite that intelligent, but sure. Let's go with that."

I was about to ask questions about demons and manifestations and other probably not-relevant things when the door opened and the two allies of Beneath entered the chip shop. Maxine immediately made a squealing noise and ran straight for Baz, wrapping her arms around his neck and planting a noisy kiss on his cheek. "Baz! Oh my goodness, where have you *been*?! So many exciting things have happened since I last saw you and—"

Mercy stood faster than I could see, drawing the knife at her belt. Before Maxine could move or say anything else in her very high-pitched voice, Mercy's knife was flying through the air and had pierced her shoulder.

Maxine let out a scream of rage and stumbled backwards with the force of the blow, her entire body slamming into the wall. Her eyes had turned to bloody red and her teeth were flashing, suddenly needle-sharp. She reached pointed claws towards Baz, who had finally realised something was going on and started to scramble away from Maxine.

Thomas let out a rumbling roar and lunged from his place in the doorway to the chip shop, enormous hands reaching for Mercy's neck. As I was in between him and his target, I got thrown bodily out of the way, landing on my injured shoulder after tipping tail over teakettle onto the floor.

"Ow," I said. Sebastian sighed agreement and went back to sleep. Some help that was. From my spot on the floor, it was very easy to see Thomas and Mercy going at it, seemingly uncaring about the destruction they were wreaking on the chip shop, my own meal now spread generously over the premises. Baz had backed into the corner by the register and was cowering with his hands over his head. Maxine had pried herself free and was stalking towards my cousin, a long needle in one hand.

I scrambled to my feet as best as possible and limped over to Baz, getting to him just before the furious and bleeding Maxine did. "Whoa, hold on," I said, holding out my hands. Admittedly, that was about all I was capable of at the moment, as my shoulder was screaming in agony and the rest of me still hadn't quite figured out up from down.

"Get out of my way, pitiful human," Maxine hissed. For a moment, I thought I saw the shadow of dragonfly wings behind her, and her skin flashed to a deep green. The moment passed, but the sharp teeth and the red eyes remained. Whatever she was—pixie, angry bug lady, some sort of nymph—she was really, really pissed. And she wanted Baz dead.

"Honestly, I know my cousin can be a handful, but there is no reason to want him dead. I mean, he's harmless!" I protested.

"Cal!" Baz yelped. "Seriously?"

"Harmless? He has betrayed our lords and aided the enemy. He has delayed our ascension and cast our lords into the abyss! When they return, they will have his head on a silver platter, and I will be the one to deliver it to them," Maxine snarled. She lunged forwards, not waiting for a response or giving me a chance to ask my many questions, and tried her best to stab Baz. I got in the way.

The needle went through the side of my neck. I don't know if it cut through one of my more important veins or if it was coated with poison or if Maxine just managed to hit the exact right spot. All I know is that I died—painfully—and came back a heartbeat later, my shoulder no longer screaming, my body aching with residual pain, and my cousin still alive.

"You shouldn't have done that," I said in a low voice. I tried to make it sound threatening, but I had never been very good at threats or intimidation. And even still alive and fully healed, my fighting skills were abysmal. I could, however, use my relative size against Maxine. I pushed off the floor with all the strength at my disposal and full-body tackled Maxine. Injured and stunned from the fact that I was not dead, she gave little resistance until we had stopped moving and I was basically just holding her down through sheer willpower.

Then, she struggled. A lot.

Her clawed fingers raked against my arms, gouging deep. Her teeth snapped inches from my face, her breath enough to fog up my glasses. She writhed beneath me and basically did her best to cause large amounts of pain so that I would let her up. I'm stubborn, though, and managed to keep her down long enough.

A moment later, and Maxine stopped struggling entirely. Her face was frozen and her eyes tracked movement over my shoulder. Mercy spoke, her words dark, "Cal, release her."

"Just kill me, aurai. I will tell you and your kind *nothing*," Maxine spat. I backed up and frowned, cleaning the spittle off my glasses.

"You should not have tried to kill Baz," Mercy said. Ah, so *that* was what set Mercy off; she had probably seen Maxine try to do something to Baz. Though, it wouldn't have surprised me to learn she had just decided to kill her for no particular reason except that doing so would balance things out.

"You are on the wrong side," Maxine laughed without humour. "You think you're so clever, getting in the way of the Rulers of Beneath. You know nothing! They will rise up and take this world and all its power and you will be crushed to dust."

"A bit melodramatic," I said. "I thought the Rulers of Beneath were evenly matched against the Rulers of Above."

"Ignorant human. You should just stay out of this," Maxine said. Before even Mercy could react, she turned her claws against herself and cut her own throat. Baz let out a whimper from somewhere behind me, then I heard the sound of retching. I didn't blame him. The few chips I had managed to eat sat uncomfortably in my stomach. Mercy cursed.

"We needed the location of that warehouse," she said, wiping her knife on a pile of napkins and sheathing it. Behind her, I spied the heaped body of Thomas—obviously dead—and had the strange sensation of disappointment flooding through my system. I hunched my shoulders and tried not to glare at Mercy.

"You didn't have to kill Thomas," I said. "He could have told us about the warehouse."

"What just happened?" Baz demanded, stumbling up to me and looking extremely pale. "I mean, they tried to kill us!"

"You," Mercy said. "They tried to kill you. While it will take some time for the giants to return from Elsewhere, information is far swifter. The bounty on your head must be getting a lot of attention."

"My head?! That chimera thing, you mean? And now this?" Baz clutched his stomach as though he was going to be sick again. "How many people are going to try and kill me?"

"I do not know," Mercy said, "but I imagine it will be many. Cal and I are in less danger, Cal because he cannot be killed and me because I can fight. The giants know this; they are not fools. They will send people after you until we all back off. Cal has already shown he will protect you."

Baz's jaw dropped and he looked desperately at me. "Cal? You have to help me! I don't know anything about fighting. I mean, last night it seemed so...but now it's real and, and...I don't know what to do."

"What we do," I said firmly, "is find the warehouse and destroy the Dragonwort. And whatever other weapons they have. Now, if they only had a phone, we could maybe figure out how to do a GPS search or something and determine where they'd been."

Mercy went over to Thomas' body and fished through the pockets, coming up with a smartphone covered in a bluish blood. I wrinkled my nose. She handed me the device and a wad of napkins and I sighed, turning on the screen.

Locked.

Figures.

"Hold on," I said, pulling out my own phone. "I

need to call someone to help me break into this phone."

"You don't know how to do that?" Mercy asked. She was glaring.

"I'm a marketer! Just because I understand social media and photo-manipulation and planning campaigns for people doesn't make me a hacker." I sniffed. "I have people for that."

Then, I video called my assistant and hoped that she wouldn't make a big deal of everything. Given how my day had gone thus far, I should have known better to even think about such hopes. Yolanda answered almost instantly and the screen of my phone was filled with her smiling face.

"Cal! I want to meet your family!"

9

———

HOME FREE

*B*az gave a tiny squeak at the sight and sound of Yolanda taking up my phone screen. Frankly, I didn't blame him; Yolanda was overwhelming in many regards, not the least of which was that she was visually slightly terrifying for the uninitiated. I had accidentally broken a man's mind when I encouraged Yolanda to reveal her full form to confirm our suspicions of the man's guilt. I had been wrong, as it turned out, but that episode ended well enough.

Anyways.

Yolanda is a rock troll, with greyish-green skin and bright, bulbous yellow eyes, a smile that could compete on any toothpaste commercial and the physique of an American football linebacker. She was large, loud, and very enthusiastic. And at the moment, she was waving furiously at Baz through the phone.

"You're shaking the screen," I admonished. Yolanda stopped waving, but her grin was hardly diminished.

"Cal, what is that?" Baz whispered quietly, staring at the screen.

"Yolanda, this is Baz, my cousin. Baz, this is Yolanda, my assistant. She's a rock troll, before you ask," I said, giving introductions. Baz gave a weak smile.

"Oh, my goodness! It is so good to meet you; Cal is often very uncommunicative about his past, and refuses to talk about his life before at all—"

"Hey! I haven't brought it up because it wasn't relevant," I said. "Besides, we were working."

Yolanda rolled her eyes. "Working. Always working. You are very grumpy, Cal. Baz, you do not look as grumpy as Cal, and I think you could probably have lots of fun. Is this accurate?"

"Um...I guess?" Baz squeaked. He cleared his throat and tried to smile wider at my assistant. He failed.

"Anyways, it is very good to meet you and I hope we will have much chance to talk in the future. But knowing Cal, he did not call to have a pleasant conversation. He wants something," Yolanda said. She said it with a smile—and knowing her, it was genuine—but I still frowned.

"I have a feeling I've just been insulted," I said. "But, yes, I do want something. We have to break into a phone and figure out where it's been. Can you do that?" I held up the phone and Yolanda made a face.

"Why is it covered in demon blood?" she asked.

"That would be my doing," Mercy said, inserting herself into the conversation and the camera frame for the first time. Yolanda became suddenly more green than grey and she looked decidedly uncomfortable. She was, as a general rule, absolutely terrified of Mercy. Actually, Yolanda was more or less absolutely terrified of just about anything that was stronger and more dangerous than she was. As she was rather low on the magical totem pole, despite having some very impressive battle magic, she avoided a great many beings.

"Oh, um, hello Mercy," Yolanda said, her voice very high.

"Yolanda." Mercy inclined her head, but it was far from a friendly greeting. "Can you break into the phone?"

Yolanda nodded. She ducked away from the camera for a moment and returned a moment later, Agravane in the frame, too. He took one look at Mercy and scowled. If there hadn't been a phone and a magical barrier that divided worlds between us, I had a feeling that things would have gotten rather complicated. As it was, Yolanda looked a little more relieved, and Mercy looked a little unsettled. Not entirely a terrible reaction.

"Okay, Cal, I need you to do what I tell you," Yolanda said. She relayed several very technical instructions and waited for me to complete each one. I was somewhat capable with technology, but I really had no idea what I was doing. Still, I managed to hit the correct buttons and after a few minutes, the phone unlocked and I was faced with a very normal looking phone with a background image of the dead Thomas and Maxine doing a selfie, looking ridiculously happy.

"They were my friends, once," Baz said quietly, looking at the picture. I couldn't tell if he was feeling sad about the new situation, or just resigned. I decided not to ask. I patted him on the shoulder and tried to smile. It was all I could offer, at the moment. Baz smiled weakly and nodded his head at the phone in my hand.

"Now I need to figure out where this phone has been," I told Yolanda. Once again, she walked me through the process and a few minutes later, we had a likely location for the warehouse full of Dragonwort. I thanked Yolanda. She just looked at me, expression more solemn than usual.

"Be careful, Cal," she said. "Family is tricky. And you've managed to get yourself into a dangerous situation."

"Again," Agravane chimed in. Yolanda nodded.

"I am merely doing my job," I said. My employees exchanged a look, and before I could say anything more, the call ended. Likely Agravane's doing, as Yolanda would have been perfectly happy to keep talking.

"Just doing your job?" Baz asked, looking as though I had thrown out his favourite shirt. "Is that all this is to you, Cal?"

I considered. "It is accurate, if not entirely complete. Death and Life sent me back because I was connected to you. You must understand, Baz, that I do not retain my emotions as normal. Sometimes I feel things, though muted, and sometimes I do not. Under such circumstances, I cannot expect to act as I used to do. You are family, therefore you matter to me. But I *am* here to do a job."

Baz just shrugged. "Yeah, okay."

Mercy looked as though she was about to say something, when a piercing noise cut through the air, wailing loudly and indicating huge amounts of trouble.

"Sirens," I said, with all the effect of the obvious.

Mercy looked around. "Where is the human?"

Baz pointed to himself.

"No," Mercy snapped. "The other human. The worker who was here?"

All three of us frantically looked around, but I was unsurprised when we found nothing. Had he even a modicum of sense, the worker would have fled when things started to turn violent. It seemed he had also called the police in the process.

"Let's go," I said. We did not even have time to wipe the place for fingerprints, though I doubted very much that Mercy's prints, or mine, were in the system. I was less certain about Baz, but decided not to press the issue. The police were the least of our worries at the moment. We needed to go to the warehouse and destroy that Dragonwort. So, we fled out the back and got as far from the chips shop as we could without drawing attention by running.

By the time we stopped and caught our breath and

regrouped, we were nearly halfway to the warehouse already. It was useful that it was in the same general area as the chip shop, but I wasn't shocked by this. It was useful to have a meeting spot that was not across town; traffic in London was terrible, no matter what mode of transport you used. A whole day could be wasted trying to get from one end of the city to the other and then back again.

Baz followed Mercy and me wordlessly, his eyes darting in every direction and jumping at every sound. He was growing paler and more nervous by the minute. Eventually, even Mercy grew exasperated.

"Will you calm down?" she demanded, rounding on Baz with teeth bared and eyes flashing, made all the more horrible by her immortal beauty. When she got into one of these moods, it was nearly impossible to forget that she was a predator. An apex predator. I stepped between Baz and the furious assassin.

"Relax, Mercy," I said. "We're fine."

"We are *not* fine." Mercy jabbed a finger towards Baz. "That fool is so nervous he is going to draw every potentially interested party right to us before we can even get there. He looks the epitome of suspicious, just when we need to blend in."

I quirked a brow and was struck with the sudden urge for sarcasm. "You're wearing a medieval dress like you've come straight from some festival. I am covered with blood of one sort or another, though most of it blends in to my trousers. Baz, frankly, looks like the most normal one here. Pray, tell, oh great assassin, what is it that is really bothering you?"

I considered crossing my arms and tapping my toe, but I decided that would beleaguer the point. Mercy let out a wordless snarl, the sort produced by those hyper-dangerous beings who more or less had a ruling say over the rest of the world, whether that world be Elsewhere or the mortal realms. She glared at me, her fiery eyes doing their best to incinerate me. It didn't work.

"Cal, just leave it," Baz whispered from where he stood behind me. "I'll do better. I will—"

"It's not you I'm worried about, Baz," I said, not once taking my eyes off Mercy.

"I should be out there dealing with this problem, setting the balance to rights so that the mortal realm does not fall to pieces. Yet here I am, playing escort to a worthless human who just happens to be related to you. Only one of *your* kin would get so deep into a situation like this." She looked as though she wanted to say more, but her jaw snapped closed and her eyes became even more furious. I had seen this once before, with her now-dead associate, Justice. He, like Mercy, was the embodiment of justice and could not go against its tenets without serious consequences. Mercy's words were far from merciful, and while she was not required to be kind, she was at least required to be true to her nature.

She apparently hated me and my kind enough to push her close to that boundary. I wondered if I should be impressed with Baz, and with myself. I settled on general annoyance.

"Baz is hardly useless," I said, brushing some imaginary dirt from my shoulder. Mercy fumed silently and I could practically feel Baz silently begging me to not bother, to not get involved. "He got us this far, did he not? Without him, we would have had no idea where to start searching for the Dragonwort. The giants would also likely be wandering around in their forms, whatever you call them. Dream projections. Manifestations. I don't care. Do you honestly think that we would have gotten this far without Baz?"

Mercy hissed through her teeth and spun around, stalking towards the warehouse. Baz shuffled his feet beside me, looking down at the pavement. "Thanks, Cal. I wish I didn't need you to defend me so much, but I really appreciate it."

"Nonsense," I said with a dismissive wave of my hand. "I speak only the truth. Besides, I am certain you will be back to your normal, gregarious and probably hugely troublesome self soon. It just takes a period of adjustment to deal with the world as it really is."

Baz scuffed his shoe again, but this one seemed slightly more cheerful. "Thanks, Cal. I can always count on you to put things in perspective," he said with a wry smile. Then, he chucked me on the shoulder and took off after Mercy, no longer quite so jumpy, but still looking around carefully. I rubbed my shoulder and trudged after my wayward cousin and the furious assassin.

This day was not turning out like I had planned.

The warehouse looked like any other warehouse, with galvanised steel siding, windows that were either high or tiny or both, a door that was always smudged along the bottom, and exactly one plant in the tiny planter outside. I think it was meant to be a tree of some sort, but it looked more like a bush than anything. There was no signage out front to indicate who owned the warehouse, but the phone's location indicated it had been there several times over the last week. As depressing as it was, this was the right place.

Mercy scouted around the perimeter of the building before she would allow us to even touch the door. When she finished, she had her knife drawn and was looking warily at the sky. "Try the door," she said.

"Not with you looking like that." I folded my arms.

"Just do it, Cal. You're the only one who can tell if there are any traps," Mercy said.

"You know, I don't actually have any magical ability apart from the whole Reaper thing, right? I'm pretty sure Sebastian doesn't know beans about traps on doors." As if to agree with me, the thing inside me yawned widely. Mercy flinched.

"No, but you can't die, so just try the door."

I had to admit, she was being rational. I slipped Thomas' phone into my pocket, shook out my hands, and touched the doorknob. I waited a heartbeat, looked around, and found myself distinctly not dead. I turned the knob. Still no death-like symptoms. Also, the door wasn't locked. I figured out why a moment later, when I actually opened the door.

I didn't die, nor did any sirens or alarm systems trigger, but there was a whooshing sound, then some very distinct, very not human growling coming from behind me. I turned around and understood why Mercy had been watching the sky.

Three large things with bat-like wings were crouched on the ground, their lips drawn back in a snarl, their claws gouging into the ground. Their skin looked almost like stone come to life.

"Hey, they're gargoyles!" Baz said, that familiar chipper tone in his voice. This was not a great time for him to be cheerful.

"Marvel at the angry monsters later," I said. "For now, inside."

"Oh, come on, Cal—" Baz started to complain.

"Not a petting zoo!" I said, just as the first gargoyle launched itself at us. Baz let out a squeak and stumbled backwards, right into me. I allowed myself to be pushed into the warehouse, then closed the door firmly.

"Cal, Mercy is still out there!" Baz screeched.

"She'll be fine," I muttered, just as there was a chorus of yips and yelps, all of them animalistic. I could have just as easily pulled Mercy into the warehouse with us and left the gargoyles to wander around the outside, but having angry winged monsters waiting for you after destroying their masters' drugs and weapon collection didn't seem like a terribly bright idea. Also, I was still a little mad at Mercy.

To borrow an American phrase: so sue me.

Of course, my logic had rather counted on the warehouse being empty, which would make it far safer than the pack of gargoyles waiting outside. Baz tapped my shoulder and I turned around to find two goons—for lack of a better word—looming a few metres away. They were hunched over and had overlarge shoulders, their necks like the trunks of trees. Their hands were curled into claws and I was fairly certain that the growling coming from their throats was producing a bass response deep enough to set off car alarms.

"Ah, yes, hello," I said with a polite wave. "Sorry to intrude, but could you show us to the loo?"

The goons looked at each other with obvious confusion. I wanted to put on my smugface, but I decided that I would settle for texting a superior treatise to Agravane later. He had informed me, in no uncertain terms, that asking directions to the loo would distract absolutely no one who was trying to kill me. I had just proved him wrong.

My smug musings, though, had rather used up my available distraction time. The goons, whatever manner of creature they might be, exchanged a glance, looked over to the clearly marked sign for the WC, and back at Baz and me. Then, they loomed even more.

"Great plan, Cal," Baz muttered.

"Well, it would have worked better had I actually used the opportunity to do something intelligent," I returned. The goons let out a couple of snarls and started moving towards us. I could have sworn that they got larger as they moved. They certainly sprouted more hair. I really hoped I wasn't dealing with werewolves.

The door behind us flew open. Literally. The door itself exploded off its hinges and flew over Baz and my heads, spinning twice and landing nearly on top of the creatures. They flinched and started moving faster. Their forms were definitely changing, but they didn't look very wolfish. More...bearish.

Werebears? Seriously?

Next time, I was definitely asking Death for a proper vacation.

Mercy stalked forwards, shoving her way between Baz and myself, covered in weird grey goo, her knife in her hand.

"Who are you?" the werebear on the left asked, though his words were gargled and difficult to understand, given that he was talking with a mouth that wasn't quite human anymore.

Mercy laughed, the sound sending shivers up my spine, despite my inability to feel terror. "Me? I am your merciful death, come to take you to the afterlife."

There was still no terror, but I was mildly impressed. The werebears, on the other hand, were not. They decided to give up on any pretence to humanity and changed fully into their bear forms. The one on the left, who had spoken, was a polar bear with massive paws, and the other was some sort of brown or grizzly bear. I wasn't very good with identifying wildlife.

Mercy swung her knife around expertly, looking as though she had come straight from an action movie. I expected a sort of prolonged, drawn out battle, or even something like what had happened at the chip shop where I distracted one of the opponents while Mercy, ah, dispatched the other. I fully expected to die again just then, perhaps even more than once. I was most certainly not looking forwards to the pain of being ripped apart by a bear.

Turns out, I needn't have worried. Mercy was apparently in a mood, or perhaps she was making up for nearly disregarding her nature earlier. She simply rushed the bears, staying directly between them, and in a few simple twists and turns, none of which I could recount with any accuracy, had drawn her knife across the throats of both creatures.

They died swiftly. If they had to die, I suppose theirs was a merciful death, being quick and likely without much pain. Still, though, the intense violence of the act made me frown. Baz sounded like he was doing his best not to retch again, though I doubted he had anything left in his stomach.

Mercy wiped her blade down with a bit of her skirt, looking distastefully at the ruined fabric as she did so. She sheathed the knife and turned to march further into the warehouse, not even bothering to give Baz and I a second glance.

"She scares me," Baz said in a voice barely above a whisper.

"Me, too," I admitted. "Come on, let's go."

We followed after Mercy through the warehouse, staying a discreet distance behind her. I looked around, half expecting there to be pallets or crates of Dragonwort, or even a place to process the drug. If not drug paraphernalia, then surely there had to be weapons. This *was* a weapons cache. The farther we went into the warehouse, though, the emptier it seemed. As far as I could tell, there was absolutely nothing there except for a card table and two chairs, where our opponents had sat before our entrance.

"Where is the Dragonwort? Where are the weapons?" I asked Baz. He shrugged.

"I mean, I never had a huge quantity, so I don't know how much there was total, but I always figured that it would be a bigger operation than this. The giants made it sound like they were furnishing a revolution against the oppressors," Baz said.

"We'll talk about your desire to fight the system another time. Right now, we need to find those weapons."

Baz and I kept searching through the warehouse, but there really wasn't much to find. Some warehouses are twists and turns of rooms for different functions, almost like a factory, and it is very easy to get lost there. Some have multiple floors, or even a catwalk. Others are just big rectangular buildings with a concrete floor. Ours was one of the latter and there was nothing here.

"Over here," Mercy called, her voice echoing through the room. Baz let out a yelp and spun around, looking for the assassin. She was standing by the only closed off space in the entire building. It was a square room made of plywood that was likely meant to be the office for whoever used the building. There were two tiny windows and a door, standing open. Mercy gestured to the interior of the room and I stepped inside.

After I hadn't been eaten or maimed or killed, Baz followed. What we saw was both a relief and a huge disappointment. The Dragonwort was there, thankfully. Or at least, a very small box of weapons. We wouldn't have to go running around the city trying to discover the dealers. However, the quantity was extremely small. A single crate was there. The dust on the floor indicated that there had not been any others there for some time.

I opened the lid and sucked in a slow breath. "Mercy?"

"Yes, Cal?" she asked, still standing in the doorway.

"I thought you said Dragonwort was a drug."

"It is. We must destroy it, and any weapons so that the giants do not get an unfair advantage and start the deterioration of the balance."

I pointed to the crate, to the objects inside, packed neatly with straw. "Those are *not* drugs. Or weapons."

"Yeah, this isn't anything like the liquid I delivered," Baz said. "I mean, I always delivered straight to dealers, and there was never a lot of it, and I stopped doing that a couple of months ago, but I figured...well, I didn't figure this."

"Let me see." Mercy pushed us aside and peered into the crate. She had only looked for half a second before recoiling and looking as though she was going to faint. For Mercy, that was really, really bad.

"What are they?" I asked.

"Dragon *eggs*," she breathed.

Ah, yes. Because things couldn't get any easier, could they? So much for plan A. Perhaps I had made a mistake in saying this wasn't a terribly complicated job.

10

CHILDHOOD HOME

*B*az actually had the sense to look around and make sure no one was approaching before saying, "That is so *cool!*"

I examined the eggs. They were about the size of ostrich eggs, with iridescent shells in a blue, a blackish grey, and a greenish purple that looked like it had come straight from the 1970s. I would have thought them just pretty, rather than assuming they were dragon eggs, but they were most certainly eggs, not plastic or metal.

I looked at Mercy, trying to gauge her reaction, but all I could glean from her expression was abject and total shock. "Is it cool?" I asked her. Baz reached out to touch one of the eggs and she nearly exploded. Mercy slapped his hand away and put the lid back on the crate, leaning over it as though we were going to steal it from her.

"Don't touch them!" she hissed. Okay, this was a

little worrying. I had never seen Mercy so insensible. So freaked out.

"On a scale of one to the end of the world, how bad is this?" I asked. Mercy flinched.

"You don't understand, Cal," she said. This was true; I didn't. "Dragons aren't like wyverns or wyrms or any thing you might have met in Elsewhere. They aren't anything like most books in popular media, either."

"How do you—?"

"I do read, you know," Mercy snapped. She pressed a hand to her head and took a deep breath. "Dragons are rare, now, because they were hunted almost to extinction a long time ago. Before the realms were separated. It was really, really hard to kill a dragon, and they placed a bloodline curse on many of the people that managed it. Eventually, Death himself had to step in and negotiate a truce."

I nodded, though I had no idea that Death was in any way diplomatic. To be fair, he was far more diplomatic than Life, but I wasn't going to bring that up just then. Mercy looked nervously at the crate, rubbing the wood with the very tips of her fingers.

"The dragons left the mortal realms because it was part of their agreement with Death. But the truth is that the barrier between realms literally can't hold them. They're too powerful. They stay away because they don't want to be bothered, they just want to tend to their studies in peace."

"Their studies?" Baz cut in, to the obvious ire of Mercy.

"Dragons are extremely intelligent, and inherently magical in a way that most beings of Elsewhere are not. They are scholars and sorcerers and they will obey no one else but Death, and that simply because they cannot harm him and give him some measure of respect. They are called Worldshakers, because their presence can shatter minds if they choose. And they are not bound by realm boundaries."

Mercy took a deep breath, and I could have sworn that she was on the brink of collapse, her nerves were stretched that taut. She looked down at the crate again, her fingers moving towards the latch. She curled her hands into fists instead. "Dragons breed but rarely, and the conditions have to be just right. Their eggs are guarded for nearly a decade against intruders, because they will bond with people who have touched the shell in a way that cannot be replicated after hatching. It's a soul bond."

This got my attention. "That would be really bad, right? If the giants got a dragon to be bonded to them? Can you tell if that's happened?" I had no idea what sort of consequences such a thing would have, but I could surmise that it would be bad. Very, very bad. Balance breaking bad, if the dragons were that powerful.

Mercy shook her head. "They have not. The shells turn gold if they have been bonded, and these are in the original state. That's not the problem right now."

"Oh?" Baz asked, a certain note of terror in his voice. "And what, exactly, is the problem?"

Mercy fixed him with a look that could have frozen over the depths of a volcano, that's how serious it was. She looked like she had done before delivering her associate Justice over to Death for punishment. That was the day she began to truly hate me. I did not want to consider what would put her expression in such a state.

"The problem is that the dragons will come for their young. They will not suffer thieves. They will happily tear this world apart to get what was taken from them."

I had a feeling that the giants were rather planning on that. It was probably why the eggs hadn't been bonded, why they were packed in an empty warehouse and guarded only by two werebears who, while dangerous, were hardly the elite of the magical world. They were more midlevel soldiers rather than the nuclear weapons. No, the nuclear weapons were coming for the eggs. That explained why we hadn't found any swords or knives or guns or anything. The eggs were bad enough.

"They wanted us to find the eggs," I said. "Or, they wanted *somebody* to find the eggs. They wanted the dragons to come rampaging in here and disrupting the realm in a way that not even the exousia could counteract. The balance would be irrelevant; the dragons would disrupt the world and make it impossible to ignore the magical beings among us. The giants would get what they wanted without once having to directly oppose the exousia. The giants are using the dragons as their weapons."

Baz clapped his hands. "Yeah, that makes sense! Tiberius knows he can't fight the angels. I mean, they cancel each other out, right? Surely he's not dumb enough to go against them directly, even if he could get a bunch of people on his side. But getting the dragons to do what he wants without his involvement?"

Mercy nodded. "This is very, very bad."

I threw up my hands. "You keep saying that, but what are we supposed to *do* about it? I mean, obviously we have to get the eggs back to the dragons. Fast. But what about the Dragonwort? Is that even relevant now? Are there other weapons out there? And we still have to imprison the giants. Can we even do that before the dragons show up?"

The aurai shook her head, cinnamon hair coming loose from its braid. Between that, the worry drawing lines on her forehead, and her blood-stained dress, this was the most upset I'd ever seen Mercy. I could have sworn that tears were shining at the corners of her eyes, too.

"I'm going to fail," she breathed. "The balance will shatter and—"

I grabbed her by the shoulders and shook her. My life was probably forfeit the moment I did, but I would recover. "Get a grip!" I shouted. I really hated shouting. It was so uncouth. "We need to to figure this out or everyone is going to die but me, and wouldn't that ruin your day?"

Mercy glared at me. "I hate you, Cal Thorpe," she said, but she wiped her eyes and straightened. She sniffled once, then straightened her shoulders and turned back to the crate. "Okay, we need to talk with Death."

I pulled out my phone and video called Yolanda. Death was loathe to carry a cell phone—he said that's what I was for—and wouldn't have answered even if he did. Yolanda, on the other hand, answered in half a second.

"Cal! Did you find the warehouse?" she asked, waving at Baz again. Baz waved back, though he still looked a little freaked out.

"I did," I said. "I need to talk with Death. It's rather important."

Yolanda winced. Agravane appeared in the frame. "Sorry, Cal. He's...away."

"Away?" I asked, a prickle of trepidation dancing up my spine. "Define away."

"Well, once he and Life sent you off to go sort out the problems there, the two of them started arguing. There was a whole discussion of Fate or something, and then they nearly tore down your office—don't worry, we got it sorted," Agravane rushed to assure me. I said nothing, waiting for him to continue. "Anyways, Life and Death got into it, and then they sort of just disappeared."

"Disappeared?"

Yolanda nodded. "Poof. Gone. We checked; Death's not at home. And Agravane even went to Life's house to see if she was there. Nothing."

"I hate that place," Agravane said with a shudder. I didn't blame him; Life's house was no place for someone so sane.

"And no one has any idea where they went?" I asked. Both shook their heads in the negative. "I could try summoning Death—"

"That won't work. Death hasn't been summoned for centuries, despite many overeager wizards trying to cross the realm barrier. There was some sort of phenomenon in the late fifteenth century that stopped up any gaps. Life and Death can cross over when they choose, but it has to be pretty big." Agravane gave a weak shrug. I wanted to groan aloud. I knew precisely the event that he was referring to. I had travelled back in time to do some relationship counselling and ended up getting an agreement from Life and Death to stop meddling in the affairs of humans.

Turns out, I am my own worst enemy. Who would have known?

"Okay, thanks. I'll try to figure things out," I said and rang off before Yolanda could ask a thousand questions. Baz had his shoulders hunched up to his ears and even Mercy was looking disconcerted.

"This is bad, Cal," she said.

"Yes, we have established this fact. In the absence of Death, what are we meant to do with the dragon eggs? Can we find a way to cross back to Elsewhere and deliver them by hand?" I asked. Mercy shook her head.

"No. The dragons live in seclusion, and they won't come out except to hunt the eggs down. They don't let anyone in."

Baz raised his hand. "Could we hold on to them for a bit? Maybe just keep them safe until we get a chance to send a message to the dragons?"

Mercy winced. She was quiet for a while, her eyes darting between Baz and me and the crate, as well as the surrounding warehouse. Eventually, she rubbed her temples. "It's the only option I can think of at the moment. I have no idea how we get in contact with the dragons, but it's better that we hold on to them than the giants."

I immediately pulled out my phone again and called up a ride share. "Right. Well, let's get the eggs back home, then we can figure out what to do with the giants."

No one argued with me. We hefted the crate to the ride share and even managed to avoid questions from the driver regarding the crate or our blood-stained clothing by saying we were practising for a Renaissance Fair. This wasn't quite the streets of Las Vegas—a place I never wanted to visit again—but it was a large enough city that we were not terribly unusual. Thank goodness for that.

An hour later, we were back home. My mother was still at work, which was a very good thing, and the house looked in tact. The giants hadn't gotten to it, nor had any of the bounty hunters laid in an ambush. We took the eggs inside and set them on the kitchen table.

"Do they need to be, I don't know, kept warm or something?" I asked. "Most eggs need some sort of incubation."

"Dragon eggs are incubated in fire, Cal. From the moment they are lain, the dragon bathes them in fire and that is enough to keep them warm until hatching. Trust me, a creature as powerful as the dragon would not have such a fragile offspring," Mercy said. She looked around. "Where are we going to put them?"

"We can put them in my room, under the bed," Baz suggested. Mercy shot him a withering look.

"Yes, let's hide the extremely powerful eggs *under your bed*. No one will think to look there!"

"Sarcasm does not become you," I informed her. Maybe it was my emotionless inflection, or just the content of the words, but I suddenly had the distinct feeling that Mercy was going to kill me. She curled her hands into fists.

"Look," Baz said. "The chimera thing that tried to kill me last night proves that the giants know where I live. Right?"

"Obviously," Mercy said.

"So they'll think I've stashed the eggs somewhere else, because I can't possibly be stupid enough to leave them where I live, because they know about it, right?" Baz was smiling, now, so pleased to be useful. It occurred to me that he'd probably had a rough time of the past couple of days. I had shown up from the dead, lost him his job, and then proceeded to galavant around the city and seek out probable death. Just because I couldn't be hurt didn't mean that Baz was impervious, even if I stood between him and danger the whole time. Baz was, unfortunately, just a human caught up in a situation where nearly everything could kill him without effort.

He was like me, when I first arrived in Elsewhere, not realising that I was invincible. Those were some of the most terrifying times of my life, and even in my current state, the memories made me shiver.

"I cannot tell if this is an intelligent plan or not," Mercy said to my cousin. "That would work, assuming that the giants and their allies believe you to be intelligent, or capable at all. But you are human, and they consider humans the most idiotic of creatures, even if they are dangerous in large numbers."

"Yeah," Baz said, sliding his hands into his pockets. As far as I could tell, he wasn't actually offended by Mercy's words at all. Impressive. "But I'm hanging out with you and Cal. And you two are obviously capable. So, assuming that they are thinking about you, not me, then they would assume you wouldn't hide the eggs here and we're all good."

Mercy looked to me in supplication. "Cal, what do you think?"

"I think that I'm confused," I said. Baz sighed. "No, not about hiding the eggs, about the weapons and drugs. Are they irrelevant? Do we just hope that the giants aren't arming their allies and expect the dragons to do all the work? It seems like they should have laid in some contingencies."

Mercy pinched the bridge of her nose and took several deep breaths. Baz and I kept silent while she did. Even without my ability to recognise other people's emotions all that well, I could tell that Mercy was seconds away from having a full meltdown. So we waited. The clock on the wall ticked loudly, each tick seeming to grow louder. And louder.

"Put the crate under your bed," Mercy said to Baz. He gave her a poor salute and rushed to do as she asked. Then, Mercy turned to me, her gaze withering and her hands on her hips. "I don't know how to find the Dragonwort or the weapons. If it wasn't at the warehouse, then it could be anywhere in the city. The world, even, though I doubt they would bother with that when the dragon eggs are here."

I nodded. "So, we disregard the Dragonwort?"

"I don't see how we have any other choice."

I could tell that this was problematic for Mercy. She liked doing things properly, and we had to ignore an element completely, even if it was tiny compared to the dragon eggs. Baz returned a few moments later, looking cheerful. He slumped into a chair and beamed at us. "What's next?"

"You don't have any other idea where the Drag-onwort could be?" I asked him.

Baz shrugged, which was not helpful. "I don't know. I mean, I only delivered a few packages for the giants, and they said it was supplements, so I couldn't tell you. And that was months ago. There hasn't been any more activity on that front for a bit. Maybe they don't have any more."

"More likely, they just decided that you were more useful serving them drinks than handling potentially sensitive deliveries," Mercy informed Baz with all the tact of an elephant. He stuck his tongue out at her.

"Okay, so we ignore the Dragonwort and hope that no one has any weapons that they can use against us," I said. "That means we have to focus on our trap for the giants."

"And how, exactly, would you suggest we do that, Cal?" Mercy asked. She folded her hands together and rested them on the table in a manner exactly reminiscent of my school headmaster. It was a little disconcerting, actually.

Baz's hand shot up into the air. "Oh, oh, I know!"

Mercy raised a brow. Her mouth tightened into a straight line. I, too, wondered what it was that my cousin could possibly suggest. While capable at school, he never excelled in strategy or long-term thinking. He was absolutely abysmal at chess.

"And how, exactly, would you imprison the projections of several highly powerful beings who could crush you with a single blow?" Mercy asked, voice dry. "Put something shiny into a box and hope they wander by?"

Baz lowered his hand. "I was going to suggest we throw Cal into a box and hope they wander by, since they hate him so much."

"Hey!" I sat up straight, struck by the strange notion that I should be offended by that. Then, I considered and turned to Mercy. "Would that work? I mean, they really do hate me. And I could act as bait, though it would probably hurt a lot."

Mercy snickered, but shook her head. "As much as I would like to witness that, it won't work. That was how they were imprisoned in the first place. They were lured into a circle of power by a Faerie, an elf, and a member of the Order of Silence, all bearing an artefact that was meant to make the bearer relatively invincible."

"Now, that is pretty cool," Baz said, a curious gleam in his eye. "Did it actually work?"

"It was a replica of the Nemean lion skin," Mercy said. "Completely useless."

Baz snapped his fingers, then brightened again. "That means it's out there somewhere?!"

"It's in an archive of the Library at Sazhem. Completely inaccessible." Mercy eyed Baz as if she expected his next question to involve a request for breaking into the library. I, on the other hand, felt a scowl coming on. It dissipated before fully appearing on my face, but I grumbled all the same.

"The Library? Those people lost the Eye of Carteria, so I doubt they have the skin anymore."

Mercy waved her hand. "It's irrelevant, Cal. It wouldn't work anyways. The giants aren't stupid enough to fall for that again. And fighting them head-on wouldn't work; they're too strong, even as only projections of their larger being."

Strong. Strong. Something in that word, along with pieces of our earlier conversation, struck a chord in my mind, like a memory of a story of a dream. I sifted through my thoughts, trying to pinpoint the idea, even going so far as to prod Sebastian awake and see if it recognised the idea. Sebastian just rolled over and went back to sleep. Helpful.

Just then, the door opened and closed with a definitive, but precise, click. My mother walked into the kitchen a few seconds later, staring down at the sleeve of her jacket in disgust. She started when she noticed all of us. Then, she coughed. "Did you have a productive day?" she asked.

"It was awesome, Aunt Teresa!" Baz leaped from his chair and held it out for her. "First we found a chips shop and then there was this battle and some dragon eggs and—"

"Basil!" My mother used the voice that brooked no argument. "Take a breath."

Baz did so, staying quiet until my mother had taken off her jacket and laid it on the table, then slid gracefully into the chair at the table. "Can you believe this?" she said to me, pointing to a tear at the head of the shoulder where the sleeve was coming away from the rest of the jacket. "I'll need to send it to a tailor and see if—"

"That's it!" I sat bolt upright in the chair, startling my mother into silence. Mercy eyed me, her gaze more penetrating than usual. I think she might have thought me insane.

"Fantastic!" Baz grinned. The grin slipped and he sat in the last empty chair. "Um, what's it?"

"The Brave Little Tailor," I said, extremely pleased with this answer. So pleased that my spine was tingling and I was near bouncing with excitement. Either that, or I was crashing without a frequent dose of coffee.

"We're doomed," Mercy muttered.

11

HOMEMADE

"Come on, Cal, we can't take this solution from a *children's* story," Baz complained. I ignored him.

"The giants have only been imprisoned once, right?" I asked Mercy. She considered for a moment, but ducked her head once.

"To my knowledge, yes. They are not fools, though, Cal. They may have been tricked before, but they will not be tricked by some story."

"They might, if we do it right," I said. Everyone, including Baz, gave me a look that probably would have been significant, or bad, had I been able to read emotion properly. As it was, I forged on ahead, ignoring the looks. "They might, if we also challenge the exousia."

This statement was met by silence. Mercy's eyes were wide and her jaw dropped. My mother simply tilted her head, mouth pressed into a firm line. Baz hunched his shoulders. "Are you sure that's a good idea, Cal? I mean, we can hardly handle the giants. And by we, I mean you, because I'd be dead twice over if they had any say in things. Do you really want to get the other side of powerful, extremely dangerous being involved?"

"Actually," my mother said, drumming her fingers on the table with slow, rhythmic movements, "it makes sense."

"Please, enlighten me." Had it not been my mother that Mercy was addressing, I would have sworn that she was hardly being respectful. But, frankly, in a conflict between Mercy and my mother, I think my mother would win. I think Mercy knew that, too.

"These two powers are on opposite sides, right? Above and Beneath? And, given the situation with the giants, they are trying to prove each other more worthy than the others, no matter that they are equally matched. This might give them a way to do that. Then, if done right, the giants can be tricked into being imprisoned again. It relies on them underestimating Cal, which seems logical, if you look at it from their perspective."

Sometimes, my mother was scary. I frowned. "Am I meant to be offended by that?"

"No," Mercy said a little too quickly.

Baz reached out and patted my hand in about the most patronising manner you could expect. "Don't worry, Cal, it's a good thing that people underestimate you. You wouldn't want to be overestimated, would you?"

Somehow, I don't think that helped matters.

I rubbed the space between my brows. "Let me at least explain to you what I'm thinking," I said. Mercy took a deep breath, eyes narrowed, but she nodded in the end. I laid out my plan, adding as much detail as I could, though most of it was vague. I think I could have added enough detail to write video games on the idea, and it still would have received the sceptical look from everybody at the table except for Baz. He was staring at me like I was crazy.

"Well?" I asked.

"It is...possible," Mercy said, carefully enunciating each word. "There is a great deal of uncertainty in it, and the likelihood of things going very badly is high. But it is possible."

"Your strategic thinking has certainly improved since you left," my mother commented. "Well done."

"Don't congratulate him until it has been completed," Mercy cautioned. My mother replied with a sharp look, but said nothing. Baz continued to stare at me like I was crazy.

"So, then, how do we contact the exousia?" I asked. "If they're angels, of a sort, do we need to go to a church to summon them? Because I haven't had a terribly good history with getting church folk to, ah, believe me."

"That is one way to do it," Mercy said, "but it's easier just to go to their offices."

That, out of everything that had been said, broke Baz out of his silence. He swung his head to gape at Mercy. "They have *offices* in London?!"

"They have offices in most major population centres," the assassin offered. "Many magical entities do; it makes it much easier when trying to communicate, or set up treaties or discuss an exchange of favours. Very few beings of significant power require summoning, anymore; the elves and some of the Fae do, but that is because they make their primary habitat in Elsewhere and..." Mercy took a deep breath, eyes closed. "Yes. The exousia have offices in London."

"Well, that makes things easy," Baz said with a cheerful smile. No one at the table, including myself, seemed to quite know how to deal with that, so we just pretended not to give each other a look and went about planning our interactions with angels.

Leaving my mother at home with strict instructions not to let anyone in, and also to be aware that there were dragon eggs under Baz's bed and they were Not To Be Touched, we went to go find the offices of the exousia. We passed through the city without incident, heading to the business district, full of tall buildings and people wandering the streets in various forms of business attire. I started recognising buildings, the steel-and-glass constructions as familiar to me as my home. My throat tightened, though I had no idea why familiar buildings would cause such a reaction.

There was the building I had passed every day on the way to work as I made my detour to the cafe on the corner, where I would buy coffee and a sandwich for lunch. That was the small Tesco where I had purchased some chocolate for a coworker's birthday. And there, with the exact same sign as before, the exact same trees growing out of the pavement, even the same black company car parked out front, was the building where my former offices had been located.

It was a tower building, holding several other offices, but on the third floor were the offices for Harcourt Marketing, where I had spent several years building up my skillset, my client base, and my reputation. I had been nearly a vice president of the firm when I had met Death in the park, and I had hardly given a thought to the place since.

But now, the ride share pulled up to the curb on the opposite side of the street and we three climbed out of the car. Mercy started towards the building—*my* building. Baz reached out to tap me on the shoulder. "Hey, Cal, isn't that—?"

"Uh-huh," I said. Had I been able to feel things properly, I probably would have had tingles up my spine or tremors in my hands. As it was, I could feel my facial muscles pulling into a confused frown. Even Sebastian bothered to open its eyes and blink at the building. I considered calling out to Mercy, but she was three steps ahead of us and already crossing through the heavy doors. So I did the only thing I could do: I followed her and tried not to think too hard.

The lobby of the building hadn't changed at all since I had last been there. There were the same fiddle leaf fig trees in sone pots at the corner of the room. The reception desk was even staffed by the same people. The pictures on the wall showed some of the same people as before, all heads of companies and celebrated people who worked at the building, hung up next to the electronic directory kiosk. It was like walking directly through my memories, except we were here and this was not a memory. It was surreal to say the least. Then, I spotted a change.

Just one change, but it set gravity to black-hole proportions. My heart pounded in my ears and my mouth went suddenly dry, yet I could have sworn that I felt nothing at all. I took a few steps over to the wall of pictures. I took my time, examining first the pictures from the Harcourt Marketing executive staff, and the executive staff for the offices on the floor below us, an innovative bio-degradable cutlery company. Then, I looked at the plaque beneath the picture I was truly interested in. It read, *In Memoriam.*

The picture was of me.

"This is really weird," Baz whispered, his voice too close. I jumped and nearly spun around to confront him, but I didn't want anyone to notice that I was there, that I wasn't dead, that I was looking at a picture of myself, only I wasn't dead.

"I hate that picture," I said. It was taken during a particularly bad heat wave in the city, when the building's air had been on the fritz. I was in my shirtsleeves, with my vest unbuttoned and my collar opened too far. I looked somewhere between annoyed and happy.

There had been a publicity scheme in the company's newsletter, highlighting the employees, and I had smiled for my picture like anyone else, only mine hadn't come out properly and no one bothered to retake it.

"You do look a little grumpy," Baz agreed with a solemn nod of his head. I wanted to tear the picture from the wall and dash it against the floor, but that would probably draw a little too much attention. So I just shoved my hands into my pockets and turned to go find Mercy, my heart pounding too loudly in my ears. She was standing near the bank of lifts, her foot tapping impatiently on the floor as she stared at Baz and me, obviously waiting for us.

I grabbed my cousin's arm and pulled him away from the evidence of my life choices, making sure to keep my head down as I passed the reception desk. Thankfully, no one noticed me, or made any connections to the person whose memory was hanging on the wall. Mercy ushered us into the lift with an imperious look, and we were almost safe, the doors closing on us with their slow precision.

Only, someone stuck their hand in between the doors and they opened again, leaving me to come face to face with my old boss and the owner of the company, Old Lady Harcourt. That wasn't actually her name, but no one called her anything different, and I had forgotten what her name actually was. Her husband had started the company ages back, and she took over when he died, giving herself a makeover and new wardrobe and turning into the picture of high-powered executive. Her hair was white and cropped short, her clothes were snappy and sharp, she had a designer purse tucked under her arm, and she wore a single strand of pearls around her neck.

Oh, and she recognised me.

I could tell the instant her brain made the connection to who I was. Her eyes grew wide and her mouth dropped open, as if she was prepared to scream. I reached out and pulled her into the lift, letting the doors close behind us.

"Calvin Thorpe!" she gasped. "You're dead!"

"Cal?" Mercy demanded with a twist of her lips. I couldn't tell if the movement was annoyed or amused. I decided not to ask.

"Not dead, it's a long story, I don't have time for this," I said, words blurring together.

Old Lady Harcourt blinked twice, and a sort of dazed look came over her face. She blinked again, then looked around at the three of us. Her eyes once more landed on me, and she gasped, in exactly the same tone as before, "Calvin Thorpe! You're dead!"

The sequence started over, with another blank expression coming over her features, only this time, she never made it to the point of exclaiming over my not being dead. The lift doors opened on the third floor and Mercy ushered the woman out before her gaze could find mine. The doors closed behind us, the lift whirring to life to take us up.

I sank back against the wall. "What was that?"

"You tell me," Mercy said flatly. "Did you know her?"

"She was my old boss," I said. "And she obviously recognised me, but...did she forget me? In half a second? Is that possible?"

"That was weird," Baz agreed, with all the helpful ability of a snarky teenager. I glared at him.

"Interesting," Mercy said, her mouth definitely turning upwards in a smile.

"Interesting? That was creepy!" I said.

"Death removed you from the fate of the world when he took you on," Mercy said. The lift doors opened again, this time on the twelfth floor, and we all exited. Well, I trudged out, but I was experiencing high amounts of grumpiness just then. "You can't just be reinserted into the world. People's brains won't be able to process it. It's a fairly complicated piece of psychological magic, and I'm surprised Death bothered at all. Well, no, I'm not surprised he bothered, just that he took it this far. I told you something like this would happen, I just never expected that particular manifestation."

"But I remember Cal," Baz pointed out.

"You're his blood. It's much harder to get rid of blood memory. But with that woman...?"

"Old Lady Harcourt," I grumbled. "She owns the company."

"Well, you could have been locked in a room with her for three days, and that would be all the reaction you'd get from her. No one you knew outside of your family will remember you, Cal. They *can't*. It would break too many laws." Mercy seemed even more amused by this by the moment. I was tempted to wipe that smile off her face, but I knew that I would be flattened before I could even try. I hunched my shoulders and shoved my hands into my pockets.

"It's not funny," I said. "I'm not even dead, and no one is going to remember me."

"I'll remember you," Baz said, clapping me on my shoulders. "Granted, no one will believe me, and I'm fairly certain that if I tell people about my cousin who died but was only working for Death, and also that there were dragon eggs and giants and such, I'll be sent to an asylum. Involuntarily."

"Thank you, Baz. That makes me feel so much better." I decided to change the subject and looked around the offices. We were in an exterior hallway that had the sign for Celestial Messenger Service next to a doorway with smoky glass and a shining gold handle. It was a little underwhelming, frankly. Nothing more than a typical office hallway, right down to the industrial grey carpet and beige walls. "So...the exousia work here? I would have expected a little more creativity than Celestial Messenger Service."

"This isn't Elsewhere, Cal," Mercy said with a very distinct roll of her eyes. "There is little need to be subtle. The humans do not require such consideration as they can rarely see what is in front of their noses."

She may have had a point, but I wasn't going to agree with her. There was little need to make me, Baz, and everyone else seem like less capable and intelligent beings than we were. I stepped forwards and opened the door, frowning at the slightly-cheap feel of the doorknob. Still, the door swung open and I stepped inside, Mercy and Baz at my back.

If I was underwhelmed by the exterior of the office, then the interior fully lived up to my expectations. While the furniture and layout of the office seemed relatively normal, the beings standing there in shining armour, swords pointed at my chest, snarls spread across their features, fit almost precisely with my expectations of "this may end badly." Thank goodness I was prepared for such things. I raised my hands in surrender and smiled as brightly as I could manage.

"Hello!" I said. My voice sounded a little artificially cheerful, so I modulated that and hoped that I was guessing properly. It was much harder to do things right when you couldn't measure emotion. "I'm Cal, and I have a business proposition for you."

12

HOME FRONT

I suppose I should have learned from my disappointment with the giants' not being gigantic; the exousia, for all they were meant to be angels, did not seem particularly angelic. That is, they looked like people, only with skin of burnished gold—actual gold, not simply a nice tan—and hair of bright copper or silver. Their armour shone with some sort of light that seemed to emanate from their skin, and beneath the armour they wore clothing that I would traditionally associate with Greek mythology. But they had no wings, no wisdom inscribed on their faces.

Frankly, the business end of the swords being pointed at me were the most convincing part of their "angelic" act.

No one spoke to answer my statement, they just stared and glared and pointed weapons at us. Baz was standing behind me, much to my relief. My mother would have killed me as many times as it took if Baz died under my watch. Mercy stood at my shoulder, looking completely relaxed, despite the fact that I held my hands in the air and there were many swords being pointed at us. This was mildly irritating, the sort of irritating that you get when a mosquito bites you and you can't itch it. I was beginning to feel an itch just between my shoulder blades, and it was mostly directed at Mercy.

"Greetings, lords," Mercy said, an unusually high amount of respect in her voice. The exousia all flicked their eyes to her, though their weapons remained trained mostly on me. "I come to you from the Order of Silence, on behalf of this emissary of Death, and his...assistant."

"The Order of Silence?" a cool voice asked. None of the sword-bearing exousia spoke, so I assumed that the voice was coming from the robed figure striding out of a corner office. He was about my height and looked no more fit to fight than I did. He was completely bald, with shining gold skin two shades brighter than anyone else. He wore a set of silvery-white robes that looked suspiciously monk-like, with his arms folded into the voluminous sleeves, a simply braided belt of leather around his slightly pudgy waist. His expression was one of serene patience, like you sometimes see in Renaissance paintings, and if I had wanted to market my coffee as a relaxing beverage that brought peace to your life, he would have been the perfect model for the campaign.

Too bad I was going a different direction with my marketing.

"Indeed, lord," Mercy said with an inclination of her head.

"And what do our sisters in balance have to say to us?" the exousia said, weaving through the ranks of soldiers until he was standing directly behind the two foremost exousia. He smiled gently. I wanted to groan in annoyance; I had forgotten that the exousia were meant to be all about order and balance. What had my mother called them? Authorities?

No wonder Mercy sounded respectful.

Unfortunately, that was not going to help our plan any. I needed to actually talk with these people, not just spout politeness over a cup of tea. Not that I would mind the tea, per se...

"I am the one who requested the meeting," I said. Mercy turned to glare at me, but she did not openly admonish me. That seemed like a good sign. The exousia took three beats to look me over, taking in my black slacks and t-shirt, my hands in the air and my very, very human countenance. I lowered my hands. The exousia soldiers tensed, their swords reaching an inch closer to me.

"And who, exactly, are you?" The robed exousia raised his brows as high as they would go. He did not look particularly impressed with me.

"I'm Cal Thorpe," I said. "I work for Death. I was sent to sort out this situation between the giants and yourself by any means necessary."

I'm not sure which of those statements garnered the ire of the robed exousia, but he narrowed his eyes at me and then, without seeming to have moved at all, he was right in front of me with his hand wrapped around my throat. He was not squeezing hard, but the mere touch of his skin was enough to send blistering pain coursing through my body. My neck *burned* where he touched, and my glasses fogged up from the steam coming off of my skin.

I coughed twice, trying to breathe through the pain, trying to stay standing upright. Sebastian writhed beneath my skin, pushing back against the burning with both eyes wide open and fangs bared. I didn't lose control the way I had with the chimera, but the exousia still exploded backwards, stumbling into the supportive arms of one of the soldiers. As soon as I was free, I doubled over, coughing.

My throat still burned, though not nearly as badly as before. I took several deep breaths, filling my lungs to capacity while activity swarmed around me, people talking in what sounded like a foreign language to my ringing ears. I vaguely felt someone put their hands on my shoulders, leading me to a chair. I sat and closed my eyes until the world stopped spinning and the pain in my neck turned to a more bearable ache.

Carefully, I reached up and touched the place where the exousia had grabbed me. It stung when I brushed my fingers over the skin, but it was not fatal. Part of me regretted that, because unless I died, I would have to heal the long way and that was often very uncomfortable when it came to magical beings inflicting injuries on me. The burning was new, though.

"Um, ow," I wheezed. Then, I opened my eyes. Baz was standing directly in front of me, his arms spread out as though to stop anyone from getting close. The swords that had once been trained on me were now aimed at him. Mercy stood just a little to one side of me, frowning, her arms folded. She was watching the robed exousia with narrowed eyes while he blinked rapidly and kept patting down his robes, as if looking for his keys.

"I must admit, I was not expecting so violent a reaction," he said with a shrug and a weak smile.

"What was that?!" I complained. My voice sounded rough and a little squeaky. I was not thrilled. "I did not attack you. I did not threaten you, or your people. Are you truly so far removed from guest protocol, or even decent behaviour, that you just attack people at random?!"

That seemed to incite a sort of furious indignation. He drew his shoulders back and lifted his chin. "I did not attack you."

"Really? Because that sure felt like an attack to me."

"Indeed, lord," Mercy said, voice low, "that was very like an attack."

"You did not come here with an appointment!" was his response. "You were therefore not under guest protocol."

"Still not a valid excuse," I said. "I haven't made any threatening gestures—"

"You invoked Death," he hissed, eyes flashing with actual light. "You insulted my people and our duty to preserve the order. You encroached on our jurisdiction."

"First of all, I *work* for Death. He is my *boss*. That was not invoking him!" I wanted to throw up my hands and stomp out of there, but something told me that would be an inappropriate response. Especially when I needed the exousia to listen to me. "And second of all, I did not insult you or your duty or encroach on your jurisdiction."

"Well, Cal, you sort of did," Mercy said in an undertone to me. "By stating that you were here to sort out the situation between them and the giants—"

"Oh, seriously! Lighten up!" I was well beyond the realm of emotionlessness at this point. My blood was well and truly boiling, and there would be no modulating this emotion. "I was sent here to preserve the balance between your two sides—by Death and Life, if you're wondering—and you're going to throw a hissy fit because you want to fix things yourself? Well, guess what, the giants have broken out of their imprisonment and are doing their best to rally their forces to turn you into a pile of ash. I think it's a little late for whatever you intend to do about it."

The exousia's nostrils flared and I was nearly certain he would try to turn me into a pile of ash again. At that point, I would very much have liked to see him try. I was pissed. Incensed. Sebastian was on the verge of roaring. I clenched my jaw and felt the blood vessel there pulsing in tune to my anger.

"Please," Baz said, in a tone of voice that was somewhere between a plea and a statement of respect. "Just hear us out. We only want to help."

The lead exousia nodded once, and the tension seemed to melt away from his body. "Very well. I, Arturo Sideria, The Star that Burns, invite you in for a meeting."

Oh, *now* the angel invokes guest protocols, right when I wanted to punch him across the face and send him to the moon. I forced a deep breath into my lungs. Sebastian growled low, the sound vibrating through my bones. But the creature coiled up inside of me and settled down to watch, one eye slitted open. I stood from my chair and brushed off my shirt. "Very good." I said.

As one, the other exousia sheathed their swords and moved into some sort of sentry formation, two lines on either side of a hallway that lead to the back of the offices. Arturo folded his hands into his robes again and glided between the soldiers. Mercy gave me a glare, then followed after him, just as graceful. Baz looked at me.

"Are we sure this is a good idea?" he whispered to me, eyeing the armoured angels with wide looks. "I mean, they attacked you for not having an appointment!"

"It's the only idea I've got," I answered.

"That doesn't actually make me feel better," Baz said. I gestured for him to precede me down the hall, while I took up the rear, ready to defend him should things go spectacularly badly. Given how this day was going thus far, I was just fine to prepare for the worst.

"Me either," I agreed.

Arturo led us into a conference room that looked, frankly, like every other conference room I've ever been in. There was a long ovular table in the middle of the room, surrounded by high-backed chairs. One wall had a whiteboard and a projector pointed at the board. The chair at the head of the table had a notepad and pen, and there was a pitcher of water with a collection of glasses that no one was going to use in the centre of the table. Arturo sat at the head of the table, his chair looking far more plush and ergonomic than the rest of the chairs. Mercy sat on one side of him, and I sat on the other, though I left an empty chair between us. Baz sat on the other side of me, eyes focused on the wood grain of the table.

"Speak, then, Cal Thorpe," Arturo said. He folded his hands atop the pad of paper, fingers laced together. I was not entirely certain I had his full attention, despite the fact that he was looking at me. Such wonderful people the control of the mortal realms were left to: the egocentric giants and the snobby exousia. No wonder things were winding down.

"As I understand it, the giants and you are opposing forces. Your natures are directly opposed by each other and you negate any effect that they bring to bear," I started. Arturo curled a lip, but nodded. "Because it is in your natures to oppose each other, though, you also come into conflict more often than not, correct?"

"The giants are beings of chaos, drawn from the dreams of magic and the unformed shapelessness that exists between the stars," the exousia said. Despite the poetical nature of his explanation, I don't think he meant the description as a compliment. "We exousia are angelic beings of order, of form and substance and purpose. Of course we are going to come into conflict with those senseless fools. We seek to guide the world. They seek to seed it with chaos, in the belief that the struggles improve things."

"Lovely," I said. Mercy hissed through her teeth at me and widened her eyes pointedly. If she was trying to communicate something to me, it failed. I ignored her. "Frankly, though, these conflicts are causing problems. Because the two of you cannot destroy one another—no matter how much you would like to do so —the conflicts escalate to beings you rule. The giants throw demons at you. You throw something equally destructive at them. Eventually, the people, *humans*, getting caught in the middle are either going to die or to notice the magic flying around. Both options, I have been assured, would upset the balance irreparably."

Arturo did not go so far as to roll his eyes, but the slight shifting of his weight gave much the same impression. "Indeed," he said, a lilt in his voice. "The giants' tactics are inexcusable. They have no concept of collateral damage, nor of preserving the mortal realms."

"You're not innocent in this, either," I said. I hadn't actually experienced the exousia's forces trying to rally, but I was pretty sure that if the giants were doing something, then the angels were doing something to retaliate. Arturo narrowed his eyes, confirming my suspicion.

"And, what, exactly do you propose, emissary of Death?" he asked, sniffing at my supposed title.

"I work for Death and Life," I said. As a marketing agent and gofer, but I wasn't going to tell *him* that. "They sent me here, and gave me the authority to solve this problem."

"You are not powerful enough to act in place of either us or the giants," Arturo said. "There is some power within you—of what sort I do not know—but it is, as far as I can tell, merely a means of self-defence. Some...trivial protection granted to you by your masters, perhaps? Certainly not enough to stabilise an entire realm."

"No, my power isn't enough," I agreed. "Nor is Mercy's. I am merely an..."

"An arbitrator," Baz offered, looking up from the table long enough to flash me an encouraging smile. At least, I hope it was encouraging.

"An arbitrator," I said. "Indeed. The power split between you and the giants was meant to keep the balance, to preserve the stability of the magic in the mortal realms. Instead, the constant fighting has caused more problems. Therefore, to preserve the future of the realm, and to keep the humans ignorant of the magical beings that walk among them and thereby avoid panic or war, two must become one."

Arturo sucked in a breath, the sound rattling through his teeth. His carefully entwined fingers came apart and he pressed his hands into the table, smoke rising from beneath them. If gold could blush, I would have sworn he did that, too. "You offer sole control to me? To us?"

"No," I said. The smoke intensified.

Mercy held up a hand. "Nor is he going to offer control to the giants."

"Then, what? I know of no other power poised to take control over the situation. There are very few even strong enough—no matter their numbers—to attempt such a thing."

"No," I said again. I smiled, doing my best to make it cheerful and encouraging. This was the smile that Yolanda had helped me practise, back when I first lost control over my emotions. She declared it acceptable. Agravane refused to tell me his thoughts. "There are not."

Arturo eyed me, his mouth twitching slightly. He said nothing. Mercy said nothing. Baz said nothing.

"I propose a series of challenges," I said, drawing my fingers over the whorls of wood in the table. My voice was light, but I had the attention of everyone in the room, despite the fact that two of them knew what I was going to do. "You and the giants compete in three challenges, with me participating as a neutral party to determine a baseline. Whoever gets the best result will be allowed to take complete control."

"You have the authority to do this?" Arturo breathed. The smoke coming from beneath his hands extinguished, and the temperature in the room dropped slightly, as if he was holding his power back just as he held his breath.

I nodded. "I do."

"Then we accept," Arturo said. I gave him that smile again.

"Very good. I shall send an email with the information for the first challenge. Until then, *no fighting the giants*. Understood?" I didn't wait for a response, just stood. I reached to tug my suit jacket straight, then realised I wasn't wearing one. I really hated having to wear Baz's clothes; he was far from a sartorial paragon. Instead, I pushed my glasses up my nose and strode from the room without a backwards glance.

"Understood," Arturo said as I reached the doorway. "Provided they do not attack us."

I decided not to answer that, as I could guarantee no such thing. My only hope was that the giants were still in transit to the mortal realms, that the dragons wouldn't show up until I could come up with a solid plan to return their eggs without injuring or killing anyone, and that my mother would let me have a late afternoon cup of coffee because I did not want to stop at a cafe on the way home.

Somehow, I doubted that all three would come to pass. I would settle for two, though, as long as one of them included coffee.

13

HEADING HOME

I've no idea how, but Mercy managed to find out the exact moment the giants returned, and also where they would be. I wanted to go find them and present the same proposal that we'd given the exousia; both Mercy and Baz decided vehemently against that. As someone on the giants' Top People to Kill list, my showing up before them would be problematic and they would likely do their best to cause me great damage, no matter how long it took. Baz was unable to go for much the same reason.

I then thought that a telephone call would be acceptable, but there are, apparently, still some things in the world of magic that cannot be done electronically. So Mercy went to go talk with the giants and Baz and I stayed home with my mother, watching television.

"What about the dragon eggs, Cal?" Baz asked while my mother was in the kitchen preparing snacks.

"I don't know. Unless we can get a message to the dragons, I imagine we'll just have to wait and then beg for our lives—and the lives of everyone else—in the hopes that they don't kill us all. Well, you all."

"Great plan," Baz grumbled.

"I can be very persuasive," I retorted. My mother chose that exact moment to return and raised a sceptical brow. "I work in marketing! Seriously, does no one understand what that means?"

"As long as you do not have to speak with the dragons directly, and can discuss the situation with them via campaign, or email, or whatever, I'm sure you'll be fine. Don't forget that interview incident back in university," she said, settling back onto the couch. Baz grabbed a handful of nuts and chocolate.

"That was not your finest moment," he agreed. I folded my arms and glared at the comedy show on the television.

The incident to which they referred was during my first-year finals at university. I had been called in to interview for an internship, and forgot that my finals were meant to happen at the same time. I ended up spouting facts from my study sheet in answer to some of the interview questions. Baz had laughed about the incident for days.

"That was simply a scheduling issue," I grumbled. "I have an app for that, now."

I imagine that the evening would have devolved into a passive-aggressive family argument had not Mercy walked in a few moments later. The relief was almost strong enough for me to feel. Then I got a good look at her. The shock at her appearance was enough to have my eyes bugging slightly.

"What *happened*?" Baz gasped, leaping off the couch and practically running to Mercy. She closed the door behind her and flipped the lock, then let her shoulders slump a little. And that wasn't even the worst of it. Her dress, which had been clean before she left, was dirty and torn. Her belt, where she usually kept her knife, was gone, and there were various scratches and abrasions up her arms and across her face. Her eyes flashed dangerously, enough for Baz to take a step back.

"The giants will be at the agreed place at the agreed time," she said, head lifted. "They accept the terms."

"Lovely," I said flatly. I rose from the couch and folded my arms. "And the cuts?"

"A minor annoyance," Mercy snapped. "Do you think me incapable?"

"Hardly. But nor are you often so dishevelled."

Mercy took one step towards me, but it was enough to have Sebastian lifting its head, taking full stock of her. Mercy glared, then tossed her head. "You are still human, for all that you have experienced and done, Cal. Do not presume to know things that you will never understand."

I said nothing. Baz said nothing. Mercy scoffed once and then strode up the stairs. A few minutes later, the sound of the shower stared up. Baz wandered back to the couch. My mother unmuted the television.

"Humans are not ignorant of pride," she murmured, eyes watching me for a moment. A heartbeat later, they flicked back to the television, but I knew that my mother understood more than she let on. I was grateful for it, at least. I settled back down as well, and we ate snacks and watched television in silence. Then, without any further discussion, we all went to bed. None of us bothered to check on Mercy.

Morning came with the particularly rousing sound of a magpie right outside my window. I had slept on the couch again and was feeling another crick in my neck, but at least no one had woken me up annoyingly early. Instead, the sun was shining, the house was quiet, and there was the distinctly marvellous scent of coffee streaming from the kitchen. That more than anything roused me and I wandered into the kitchen without having put on my glasses. What I found would have confused me had I been able to see properly, but as a collection of blurry dots, everyone sitting politely at the table was simply startling.

"Are you wearing jeans?" I asked Mercy.

"Put on your glasses, Cal," my mother said. I did, cleaning them on my shirt, but when I put them on the scene made just as little sense as it had with them off. Mercy was indeed wearing jeans. Baz was wearing something that looked almost like business casual, but the stain on the shirt collar didn't help much. My mother alone looked normal, with a 1930s style vintage suit on, hair coiffed and expression serene.

"Am I late?" I poured myself a cup of coffee, took a tentative sip, and nodded appreciatively at my mother, since Baz had obviously not made the beverage. "Is there breakfast?"

"I have been up for several hours, finalising your plans," Mercy said with a distinct frown, ignoring my comment about breakfast. I did not need to be adept at reading emotions to know what that meant. And indeed, even as I thought it, Mercy continued. "You do realise that if this goes wrong, which it has the high probability of doing, then you are condemning the mortal realms to whomever wins your ridiculous challenge."

"Hey," Baz protested. "You were just fine with this plan yesterday. If you weren't, then why did you go ahead with it?"

"I went ahead with it because there did not seem to be any alternatives. There are still no good alternatives, not unless you wish to sacrifice most of the people of this realm. But just because I do not see any alternatives does not mean that I think this will work." Mercy took a sip of her coffee and pointedly stared out the window. Baz made a face and probably would have stuck his tongue out at Mercy had not my mother cleared her throat pointedly.

"Well, we have about an hour before we need to be there to meet the giants and the exousia. We should probably leave a little early, to head off any potential—"

"All the preparations have been made, Cal," Mercy snarled with more venom than I had heard from her for a very long time. Whatever had happened the night before that left her abraded and injured was obviously still weighing on her, despite the fact that her immortal body had healed the injuries. Pride indeed. I knew that no matter what I did, no matter if we managed to pull this off, no matter if we restored the balance or save the world or what ever, Mercy would never like me. She hated me now, but you can hate someone and still like them. It is rare, but it is possible.

After all this was said and done, I doubted Mercy would ever find it in her to do anything but loathe me.

We finished breakfast without any further discussions, then left, my mother staying home to guard the eggs, and also because it was Sunday and she didn't need to go and work. Had it been any other day of the week, I imagine the eggs would have gone with her, or remained at home. There was little that got in the way of my mother and her work. I knew I should have been worrying about the eggs, knowing that the dragons would come, probably sooner rather than later considering my luck, but I could not bring myself to face that particular challenge. I had no solution to the dragons, so I did not think about it. Instead, I focused on the challenges for the day and hoped that things would not go too badly. That was, after all, why I was the "neutral" party, the baseline, the mortal participating in the challenge.

Also because if anything went wrong, I was the only one not going to walk away with permanent damage.

When I got back to Elsewhere, I was going to have a conversation with Death about the nature of my work. We really needed to renegotiate my contract.

The park was mostly empty, which was precisely why we had picked it for the meeting. We didn't need innocent bystanders getting involved. There was a small table set up under a grove of trees, holding a scale model of the city. Mercy had done well under such short notice, even getting a second table with pitchers of water and some glasses, along with several chairs set up. Neither the giants nor the exousia were here, yet.

We sat at the table, conversation between us nonexistent. A few minutes later the leader of the giants, Tiberius, arrived. He had not brought a retinue like I expected, simply showed up alone and with swaggering stride. He wore a leather breastplate over a linen shirt of some sort, and what looked to be a leather kilt, though I imagine that it was meant to be more Roman than Scottish, given the short sword at his belt. Unfortunately, whoever had sold it to him included the flask that went with a Scottish dress kilt, complete with cow-skin cover. Baz did his best not to snicker.

Tiberius sneered at us, but he clapped his fist to his

chest and gave a perfunctory nod of his head, probably some minor show of respect for our various positions, even if he did not like it. I was, technically, offering him sole control of the mortal realms. That apparently counted for more than his loathing of me.

"Have a seat," I offered. The giant sat in one of the plastic chairs, the material creaking under his weight. "I trust you were not too inconvenienced by your return journey through Elsewhere?"

Tiberius curled a lip. "I have been around for longer than you can imagine. A few days travelling through Elsewhere to a waypoint was hardly anything at all."

"I'm glad," I said. "You are aware that trying to kill either me or Baz or Mercy would be an automatic disqualification, correct?"

The giant ground his teeth and I could have sworn that the blue skin over his cheeks darkened slightly. "Your messenger made such things very clear last night."

Mercy pointedly ignored me when I looked at her. The cuts had been healed and she looked, for all intents and purposes, like a normal person having a day in the park. Well, excepting the immortal grace and beauty and deadly intent that was impossible for her to hide. I returned my attention to Tiberius and nodded.

"Good," I said, and was about to say more when the giant lay his hand flat on the table and leaned in.

"Do not mistake me, human. Once I prove my

worth over that of the exousia, then you and I shall have a score to settle. But until then, you are far too useful to me, and I will not disrupt these plans. Our truce is temporary, at best."

Had I been anyone else, or even myself under different circumstances, I'm fairly certain that the gaze Tiberius levelled at me would have had me quaking in my shoes. As it was, I simply blinked and turned to Baz. "I do believe that he is trying to intimidate me."

"Probably," Baz agreed. Tiberius growled low in his chest and my cousin threw him a beaming smile. "So, should I stop by the bar for my last pay cheque, or will you put it in the post? I didn't get to ask last time I saw you."

Tiberius surged upwards, fury flaring his nostrils and his movements snapping off one of the legs of the chairs. Mercy coughed, once, without looking at the giant, and he deflated, though his eyes still sparked with imminent threat. He was about to sit down in a different chair when a brightness appeared from the edge of the park. Immediately, Tiberius drew his sword and levelled it towards the approaching light. Mercy coughed again, this time twice, but the giant did not back down.

"That would be the exousia," I said. "You are under oath, if you remember?"

"I need no reminder, human," he spat. The sword was sheathed a moment later, and Tiberius faced the exousia with arms folded across his chest and his legs spread wide. Wonderful. I rolled my eyes. Posturing.

The exousia that approached was Arturo, also without retinue. I was not entirely sure what this meant, that both would arrive without support. I suppose it was to do with arrogance and more posturing; if they could face each other without support, they were displaying their prowess, their strength. It was silly, but I wasn't going to complain. It made my job much easier.

"Hello," I greeted Arturo. He wore the same robes as the day before, his hands concealed in the voluminous sleeves and a serene expression on his face that I have no doubt was for Tiberius' benefit. "Please, have a seat."

Neither giant nor exousia sat.

"Let me rephrase," I said with something hinting at annoyance. "Sit. Now."

They sat, taking chairs and placing them at opposite sides of the table. I resisted the urge to roll my eyes again. Baz snickered. Arturo and Tiberius stared at each other in silence, neither appearing willing to break the gaze and thus admit defeat.

"Ahem. Can we begin?" I asked, resting my elbows on the table. Arturo looked at me, the beginnings of a smile curling at the corners of his mouth.

"How is your neck doing? It seems to be better than it was yesterday," he said. I tried not to scowl; I had almost managed to forget about the wound on my neck. It had indeed healed a little bit, turning from an angry red to an itchy splotch that wrapped around my throat. My mother had offered calamine lotion, which had done nothing at all.

"Mercy?" I asked through my teeth. The aurai did not hesitate, rising from her seat as though carried on a breath of wind. Even in jeans and a loose shirt, she conveyed exceptional deadliness that one could not find in the mortal realms. Her expression was calm, impassive.

"We summoned, you came. Thus will it be that this council, lead by Cal Thorpe, emissary to Death, decides the fate of the mortal realms. This decision will be based on three challenges, to measure speed, strength, and intelligence and thereby determine the most worthy to claim rule over this place. The participating parties are Tiberius, of the dreaming giants, ruler of Beneath. And Arturo, of the exousia, ruler of Above. Cal Thorpe will participate as a neutral party, a baseline against which your skills will be measured. The rules are as follows," Mercy spoke, her voice clear and cold. She looked at me for a brief moment, then continued. "One: you will complete the challenges under your own power. There is to be no assistance from outside, nor no supplemental power added to your own. Two: there will be no interference with any of the competitors, either by yourself or others, nor no interference with myself as judge, or Basil Thorpe, as judge. Three: no decision about the division of the mortal realms shall be made until all three challenges are complete, either by yourself, or others. Do you understand all of these rules as I have stated them, and do you agree to abide by them?"

Tiberius slammed his fist into the table, making two of the water glasses jump. "I do!" he roared, voice shaking the ground.

Arturo merely smiled slyly and gave a slow nod. "I do."

"I do," I said, for good measure. Mercy nodded.

"The agreement struck, the first challenge shall begin." She stepped away from the table and went to go stand by the other table. The rest of us followed, once again Tiberius and Arturo standing on opposite sides of the scale model of London. Baz stood just behind Mercy. She spread her arms.

"The first challenge is speed," she said. "You must circle the city twice. The first to do it shall be determined the winner. Baz will note down the times of each individual, and I will determine the winner should the times be too close to call."

Tiberius laughed, tossing his head back and pressing his hands to his belly. Even Arturo seemed amused, though he pressed his mouth tight and glared at Tiberius' display. Eventually, the giant calmed and wiped a false tear from his eye. He nodded at me. "You intend to circle the city twice?"

"I am the neutral party," I said. "I am to participate in all the challenges."

"This will take ages!"

I shrugged. "Then it takes ages. You agreed to the challenge."

"Oh, I do not mind watching you humiliate yourself, but it seems so pointless when I know that I will beat you easily. The exousia, too, will thrash you soundly, I believe is the phrase. You humans struggle to run even marathons!" Tiberius snorted.

I surreptitiously checked the time on my phone. "Well, we'd better get started, then. I would like to be home for supper."

Mercy's jaw clenched and her eyes flashed, but a blink later and she was as calm as ever. Neither Arturo nor Tiberius commented, or even seemed to notice. She folded her arms before her. "Baz, do you have the timers set up?"

Baz nodded and held up his phone, an app open with a zeroed timer.

"Then, as I count to three, you will begin. One, two, three!" Mercy raised her hand into the air. Tiberius and Arturo sprang away, each going in a separate direction, their feet flying. The exousia was the faster, by which I mean he blurred from my sight after only a few seconds. Tiberius bounded away like a stag, each step he took making the ground rumble. I looked at Baz, then at Mercy, and calmly walked around the scale model of the city.

Twice.

14

NO PLACE LIKE HOME

"*W*ell, Cal," Baz said with a manic grin. "I think you could have done better than thirteen seconds. But I suppose it will do."

Mercy scoffed and folded her arms. "This is wrong. Not in the spirit of things at all."

I shrugged and sat down, putting my feet on the table and leaning back in my chair. "That's rather the point. I completed the set task, and I did it fastest. It's not my fault that the others interpreted things differently."

"You cheated," Mercy snapped. She threw up her hands. "I know this was the plan, but it is still cheating."

"It's called being smart. The instructions never specified *which* city to circle, the scale model or the real thing," I said. "Now, do you think we'll have time for lunch before they get back?"

As it turns out, we did not have time for lunch,

though it was a near thing. Arturo appeared first, his skin a flushed blaze of light, his steps trailing fire in his wake. He stopped before the table, breathing heavily, and Baz called out his time.

"Two hours and seventeen minutes and thirty four seconds," he said, staring at his timer. "Impressive. Twice around?"

"Twice," Arturo said, thrusting his chest out with pride, his breath still heavy. For the first time, though, he seemed to realise that I was sitting there, not running around the city and trying desperately to catch my breath. "You...have you completed the task? Already?"

I nodded. Baz was about to give my time when the ground trembled, leaves falling from the trees as Tiberius thundered into view. He was breathing much heavier than Arturo had been, but that's what you get for trying to race someone who had starfire in his veins. The giant was sweating, his white hair closer to grey with the moisture. His leather armour looked uncomfortably warm and his breathing was a rattling wheeze. He glared at Arturo and bent over, hands on his knees.

"Two hours, eighteen minutes and one second," Baz said, noting the time. He looked up at Tiberius. "The slowest of the three times," he said, not sounding at all apologetic.

"The human was here when I arrived," Arturo said, looking sideways at me. Tiberius straightened and gaped, eyes bugging, chest still heaving for breath.

"Truly?"

"Truly," Mercy said, voice just as flat as it had been when describing the rules. She did not look at me. "Cal's time was thirteen seconds."

"Impossible!" Tiberius roared, the sound enough to wobble the pitcher on the table. It held together, barely, but I reached out a hand to steady it.

"And yet, I declare Cal to be the winner," Mercy said.

"You are on his side," Arturo snapped. "You have obviously ruled in his favour."

Mercy stood from her chair, shoulders back and eyes blazing. She stared the exousia down. "I am Mercy, of the Order of Silence. I am an architect of balance. I do not do anything that would jeopardise the balance. And you have the gall to accuse me of ruling unfairly?"

Her voice sent shivers down my spine, and I was not even the target of her tirade. Arturo blinked and looked away. He took a deferential step backwards and inclined his head. "Forgive me, my lady," he said.

Mercy said nothing, only shifted her gaze to Tiberius, who was still striving to catch his breath. He jerked his head in some poor imitation of Arturo's respectful nod. "You are deemed impartial," Tiberius said.

Mercy ground her teeth together, but sat. "The next challenge will be one of strength. Meet here tomorrow at dawn."

She waved a dismissive hand and the giant and

exousia vanished, as if they had not even been there. I fingered my water glass, studying her for a moment. Mercy looked weary, more than just the usual strain of having to deal with me.

"Is this...problematic for you?" I asked, measuring my words carefully. "To...arrange things like this?"

Mercy scoffed and slumped back in her chair, the first time I had ever seen her so relaxed, even if she was scowling. "Despite what you may think, Cal, I am always acting in service to the balance, and to my nature. Your tasks are...necessary to the preservation of the balance, and you have not changed that, no matter your particular means of interpretation."

I wasn't sure whether to be relieved by that or offended. Or both. I settled for sipping at my water.

"Say, Cal?" Baz asked. "Um, how, exactly, are we going to arrange tomorrow's challenge? Today was relatively easy, but a feat of strength? It's a little more difficult to...you know. Bluff."

I placed a hand on my chest and acted hurt. "Bluff? I'll have you know I do not bluff! I went around the city. Twice. Exactly as I said I would."

Baz shrugged. "You know what I mean."

"Three stations," I said. "I ordered the supplies last night, and they should be here by six in the morning tomorrow, just as planned, though I doubt Death will appreciate the bill for such a rush job. As long as we keep the others from interfering in any way, then it should go just as we intend."

The looks I received from Baz and Mercy were a

little skeptical, but neither argued the point. I don't know what I was expecting. Maybe some sorts of congratulations, or at least an acknowledgement of my success. I had been fond of being lauded for my accomplishments back in my previous life, in so far as I enjoyed reaping the rewards of a job well done. Since working for Death, I was mostly pleased to just survive each day with my sanity intact. Though, whether I was still sane was a subject up for strenuous debate. I knew that my marketing was relatively successful; the numbers were proof of that. And I had managed to accomplish several tasks that were very much not in my job description, but there was little joy in accepting praise.

The world felt harder and crueler since I had started working for Death. Maybe I was just waking up to the reality of things, becoming aware of the true nature of the world. I didn't need praise in the midst of all that.

There was still a part of me, though, that wanted the approval of my family. I hadn't known it until coming here, and facing the unequivocal joy with which Baz greeted me, and the generally pleased reception from my mother. Now that Baz looked weary, tired and worn and not nearly as pleased to have me around, I found myself longing for his approval.

There's one thing that I know, though. You can't go back to the way things were. Time is persistent like that, and I've met the guy, so I know what I'm talking about.

I couldn't go back home and expect my life to fall into place as it had been before this mess. I would happily settle for making Baz's smile come back, whatever it took.

We went home and Baz slumped into the couch, flipping on the television and staring blankly ahead. Mercy left us to ruminate on whatever she was ruminating on, which I would probably need to deal with eventually. I sat next to Baz.

"Hey," I said.

"Yep," Baz said, flicking through channels.

"What's going on?"

My cousin threw my a look, both insulted and a little hurt, then turned his attention back to the television. He shrugged one shoulder. "Oh, you know, just trying to keep the whole world from turning into a big puddle of destruction."

"If that were all, you'd be doing so with a grin and a plan," I said. "I remember full well the incident with that chocolate bar and the bookstore. How long before you're allowed back in?"

There was a hint of a smile on Baz's features as he recalled the incident. "Another two years, I think."

"See? So what's going on, Baz, and don't give me some save the world crap." I folded my arms and pretended to glower, but really my mother does that much better than I do. Instead, I pushed up my glasses on my nose and studied Baz.

He flicked through another couple of channels then turned off the television with a half-hearted snarl.

"I don't know, Cal. Just…one day, I'm living my life, working for people I thought I was helping, trying to get over you dying and leaving me behind and then, well, you're back. Not dead, thank you very much, and oh by the way, Baz, you let out a group of magical beings that could squish the world into tiny pieces and I'm here to fix it. Okay, fine, I made a mistake in helping the giants. It's been known to happen. But I always fix it, and now I can't do that. I can't do anything."

"You led us to the warehouse," I pointed out. "You helped us recover the dragon eggs before they could be bonded or sold or planted somewhere the dragons would do the most damage. You've provided intel and you are helping us get the giants back under control, and the exousia, too. How is that doing nothing?"

Baz rounded on me, expression thunderous. For the first time in my life, I saw the fire beneath the easygoing exterior that Baz showed the world. His eyes burned and I pitied whoever stood in his way. Oh, wait, I did.

"Great," he snarled. "I led you to a warehouse that you likely could have found on your own, even if it was just a little slower. And on the way, you stood in front of me while people I knew and trusted tried to kill me. Mercy dismembered them, and those others guarding the eggs. You're the one who came up with the plan to fix things, and I just get to sit on the sidelines, providing moral support. You don't need me, Cal. I'm contributing nothing! I can't fight, I can't do magic, I can't even provide intelligent ideas. Why did you even come back, Cal?"

I answered without hesitation. "I came back because you're my family, Baz. And I would be just as helpless as you if it weren't a mistake that Death lost my soul. I can't fight worth anything, no matter how hard Agravane has tried to teach me."

Baz scoffed and sank back into the couch, his fight gone. "You're still the one with the plan."

"Well, yeah," I said. "I've always been the one with the plan. Neither you nor I would have made it through school if that weren't the case. That doesn't make you any less valuable, Baz. You're good people, and you are not worthless. Never worthless. Think of how depressing my life would be without you."

My cousin frowned. He ran his fingers over the buttons of the remote, but didn't turn the television on again. "You might be the only one who thinks that, Cal," he said, barely louder than a whisper. I waited, and Baz took a deep breath. "Aunt Teresa is my very last chance. I've been kicked out of my own family, and she was the only one who offered me a place to stay. I haven't been able to hold down a job for longer than six months, and the jobs I've gotten are either just this side of shady or pay less than dirt. I have no prospects, no future, hardly a life now. When I was working for the giants, they were my only friends, and you saw how they treated me. Without you around...well, let's just say that things have been bad for a while."

"I didn't mean to leave like I did." I remembered

vividly the terror that had gripped me when Death first appeared, knowing that this was my only way forwards, that everything I had known would have to be left behind. Even without a soul, that memory remained perfectly clear, the emotion louder than anything I had felt for a very long time. "I wouldn't have done so had there been a choice."

"Yeah, but look at you now, Cal," Baz said, smiling weakly at me. "Working for *Death*. You singlehandedly built a marketing empire in Elsewhere, and by your own description, you've saved the world more than once."

"When did I say that?" I frowned, trying to recall my words.

"You stood between Life and Death in the middle of the Italian Renaissance," Baz stated, counting off on his fingers. "You solved a murder that would have caused a rift between Life and Death, potentially starting another world war. You kept Faeries from going to war, you faced down Al Capone reincar-nated...should I go on?"

"No," I said. I pinched the bridge of my nose. "I really need a raise."

"I'll say," Baz snorted. He sobered. "Seriously, Cal, this work, this life you've crafted for yourself, it suits you."

"Thanks, I guess," I replied. "It's really not as glam-orous as you make it sound. If I could feel things prop-erly, I likely would have screamed my way through half of those situations."

"Perhaps," Baz said. He smiled. "Perhaps not. You're not the same Cal that went away, no matter if you can feel things or not. You're...better, stronger."

"I'll take your word for it. I'm afraid I'm not an impartial judge. But all that aside, Baz, you'll find your place, too. You're capable, truly. Just...be patient. Life is kindest to those who fight her."

Baz shuddered. "That kind of freaks me out, you know. She sounds terrifying."

"You have no idea," I said. And with that, we settled in and watched the television, the silence between us comfortable once more. There were probably loads of details that needed to be worked out. My plan for sorting out the situation between the giants and the exousia was fragile at best, and then there were the dragons to think about. But just then, even with all we had yet to face, it was nice to sit on the couch and watch television with my family.

It felt almost...normal, which was such a strange sensation that I had to turn it over in my head for a while. I knew that whatever was to come, it would be okay. Because while I couldn't go back to the way things were, I wasn't entirely disappointed with how things had turned out.

15

STAYING HOME

I would never consider myself a party person, nor did I have much of a social life these days, as my social events usually involved Agravane and Yolanda, a giant tub of popcorn, a cup of coffee and whatever soap opera was available on television. Back when I was, well, normal, I would occasionally go out of an evening, but I was always back well before morning. So when I tell you that I would much rather be up late at night and well into the wee hours, rather than waking up first thing, take me seriously.

I woke to Mercy kicking my arm, which dangled off the edge of the couch. I know that it was Mercy because she was firm in her kick, but not cruel. It wasn't in her nature to be anything close to cruel, since she was literally the embodiment of mercy. Baz would have just waved a cup of coffee beneath my nose, and my mother would have just cleared her throat. Loudly.

No, Mercy, for all her merciful nature, had to kick me. I can't say I was surprised.

I cracked open my eyes and found myself faced with a blurry image of the assassin standing over me with her arms crossed. I imagine she was glowering at me, too, but I wasn't wearing my glasses and couldn't tell.

"Seriously?" I grumbled. "It's still dark out."

"You wanted to be woken," she sniffed. "I woke you."

"I figured it would be a reasonable hour, preferably with coffee and breakfast involved. Not...do I even want to know what time it is?" I sat up and rubbed my eyes, fumbling around for my glasses and phone. I looked at the time on the screen and sighed. "Four in the morning. Why?"

"For a being who is incapable of feeling emotions properly, you are very grumpy," Mercy retorted, completely ignoring my question.

"Yes, well, you should have been around when I first lost my soul and was behaving, how did Yolanda put it? Like a particularly chatty Vulcan?" I stifled a yawn. "We don't have to be at the park for another three hours."

"We have to supervise the delivery." Mercy delivered me another kick, just to be sure I was getting up, then stalked away. Baz wandered into the room, his hair sticking up in all sorts of directions, holding a cup of something that smelled suspiciously and marvellously like coffee.

"Well, I can say this, Cal," he rasped, "you really have charmed her to pieces."

"If you're being sarcastic, then I've missed the point. Coffee in the kitchen?" I slid off the couch and stood, straightening out muscles that were unappreciative of the upholstered furniture. Baz jerked his head towards the kitchen and started shuffling off, presumably to go get dressed.

I managed a full two cups of coffee before Mercy demanded that Baz and I get into the ride share waiting outside, so we could head to the park. I didn't particularly want an argument, so I went without protest, though I don't imagine I looked much more awake than Baz did; he was wearing his band t-shirt of the day backwards and had dark circles under his eyes. Mercy sat there looking perfectly composed, except for the folded arms and the scowl.

"I imagine you are rethinking your decision?" Mercy asked when we were about halfway to the park.

"What decision?"

"All this foolishness?" She waved her hand expansively, as if she were describing my whole life. Given the current situation, I wasn't entirely convinced that was a bad thing.

"I assume you mean the eggs, since we have already discussed the challenges and came to the conclusion that they were our best—or rather, *only*—option. Or did you come to some glorious revelation while we were asleep?" I asked. My tone was entirely sincere, though I was intentionally trying to be sarcastic. Baz blinked at me, still lost in the throes of morning confusion. Mercy glared.

"I don't understand you," she snapped. "You have the opportunity of several lifetimes, working for Death and Life, and being what you are. Yet you seem to completely ignore your responsibilities and you treat serious situations with flippancy and arrogance."

"Being what I am?" I sighed and shook my head. "I did not choose this, Mercy. I did not ask to be a Reaper. It simply happened. A mistake on Death's part and some ill-timed vacation, a favour for Life, and it just happened."

"So, what, you're going to disregard your duty? You're going to—"

I narrowed my eyes, and Sebastian woke up, far more attentive than I was feeling, even with two cups of coffee streaming through my system. Sebastian lifted its head and focused all its attention on Mercy. "In what way am I disregarding my duty?" I asked, a growl reverberating through my chest. The ride share driver looked askance at us through the rearview mirror.

"Cal, you might want to tone it down," Baz muttered, suddenly more awake. Sebastian snorted in response, but lowered its head again. It remained aware.

"You're treating the entire balance of the mortal realms as though they were a children's story. You're relying on luck and lunacy and cheating to get what you want. There are ways of doing things, and you don't seem to use a single one of them."

Mercy seemed to want to rehash several different arguments at once, or maybe she just woke up with her loathing of me refreshed by our shenanigans the day before. Either way, it was unhelpful and would likely interfere in our task for the day if she let it fester further. If *I* let it fester further.

"The way of doing things that you're referring to," I said in my best accent, with the most precise language, all picked to show Mercy that I was not a bumbling fool, "has resulted in many deaths, wars, and I cannot even begin to describe how many people being generally mistreated. If we were doing things the way they were 'meant' to be done, then my entire home would be destroyed several times over. The entire mortal realms would be destroyed. Life and Death would have obliterated this place, Justice would have ruined the balance you're so fond of—"

"How *dare* you bring him up?" Mercy snarled. I simply fixed her with a firm look and shook my head.

"You can hate me all you like. I won't stop you, nor blame you. But I can do nothing to change what has been, and you have provided no alternatives to the situation at hand. So either contribute, or keep silent."

Something seemed to break in the depth of Mercy's gaze. She shuddered once, the movement settling into an eerie preternatural stillness. She looked away.

"Cal," Baz said, the admonishment in his voice obvious even to me. He was right, too.

I reached out and took Mercy's hand, wrapping her fingers firmly in my own, preventing her from moving away. "What happened to Justice, not being a Reaper, even this stupid situation with the giants and the exousia...None of it is your fault."

Mercy pulled on her hand and still did not look at me.

"None of it," I insisted.

Mercy still did not look at me, and had she been anyone else, the shining in her eyes might have been tears. I released her hand and she scooted as far away from me as possible, which wasn't far in the tiny car. Before I could say anything else, and probably make things worse, we were at the park. The three of us decided, by some silent, tacit agreement, to just get on with things. If we made it through, we would talk things over. Or not.

Thankfully, the park was once again completely empty. I don't know how Mercy managed to arrange for people to avoid the place, but it was useful to not get innocents involved. The only people at the park were the people making the delivery, and even they were almost done. I stayed back while Mercy talked with the delivery people. They seemed to ask her some sort of question, and she pointed at me. I waved half-heartedly to the people. They stared for a moment, then shook their heads and shrugged, leaving everything as requested and driving off in their lorry.

"What was that about?" I asked Mercy, walking around the items.

"They wanted to know what was going on," she said, voice dry. "I told them you were an artist doing a sort of performance art installation and that you were going to make loads of money out of it."

Baz looked at the three items, all identical except for the materials, and snorted. "There's no way anyone would make money off of this."

"Thank you," I grumbled, but he was probably right. The statues, for that was what they were sold as, looked like, well, something you might buy off the side of a road or at a gardening centre. Lawn art. Made of concrete. By a toddler. Okay, they weren't that bad, but they were just lumps of concrete that were—I think—meant to be bears. Or rabbits. They were placed on pedestals that secured them to the ground and stood about seven feet high. Two of them were solid, with the marble bases being secured to the statues with steel rebar. The third, while completely identical in looks, and also standing on a marble base, was made of styrofoam.

Yep, I was going to cheat again. This time in more than just interpretation. Mercy might have had a point; cheating in such an important situation was hardly sporting, but I honestly couldn't think of a different way to do things. Not unless we wanted to wake Sebastian up again and see what happened.

I nudged each of the statues to be sure they were secure, and Baz gave me a thumbs up. "Looks good. Honestly, I can't tell the difference at all."

Mercy opened her mouth, frowning, but shook her

head and said nothing, only set up the table and chairs again. "They'll be here soon."

I don't know why, but her obvious disappointment caused just a twinge of hurt, right in the centre of my chest. I rubbed at the spot and the feeling went away. Of all the times to have an emotional response, now was certainly not the time. I had to focus. I had to make it through this and keep either Tiberius or Arturo from figuring out what was going on.

Yeah, like I had ever thought this would be easy. I should know better than to tempt Life by handing her a line like that.

As if the mere thought of the giant and exousia could conjure them, both appeared in the park at the same time, walking towards us from different directions. They looked wary but confident, and once again they hadn't brought any of their people with them. Good.

"What is this?" Tiberius asked, frowning impressively at the statues. "Are they meant to be gorgons?"

"Bears, I think. Or rabbits," I said. "I didn't really ask."

"Why in the world have you brought bear statues to the park?" Arturo asked, his expression almost exactly like Tiberius's, only more so. "They're an eyesore."

"Yeah, well, we had a budget," Baz said folding one arm and squinting at the statues, as if that would improve their appearance. "There's only so much you can expect from budget statuary."

"Good morning," Mercy said, cutting through our budding discussion of bad art. We all wandered over to the table, which was set up with three swords laying out in a line. "This is the second challenge, meant to determine strength. As you can see, we have provided three statues upon which to test your strength. Each statue is meant to represent potential opponents that you might face in the ruling of the mortal realms. The swords are to be your weapons. You must take the sword and stab it through the centre of your statue. The one who impales the statue the deepest will win. You may not use magic to alter the sword or statue in any way. Are there any questions?"

Baz raised his hand, a cheeky grin on his face. Mercy snarled at him. "About anything *other* than the appearance of the statues."

Tiberius and Arturo shook their heads. Mercy nodded. "Arturo, take your sword. You will be attacking the statue on the left."

The exousia lifted a sword and grinned like a feral cat. He gave a few experimental swipes with the shining blade, gripping the hilt first in two hands, then one. He tested the edge with a finger and nodded in appreciation when a single drop of shining blood welled from the slender cut. They weren't proper antiques, I knew, but Mercy had done well in finding a sword smith in modern London in less than two days.

"Get on with it," Tiberius said, feigning a yawn. "Or are you not sure you can handle the task?"

"Only a fool attacks without first understanding the

weapon he uses," Arturo said with a dainty sniff. He lifted his chin then gave a gracious nod to Mercy. "You have chosen your tools well."

Baz choked back a laugh. I whacked him over the head. "Not helping."

Arturo studiously ignored us, straightening his shoulders and sliding his feet into some sort of martial arts stance. He approached his statue, expression turning thunderous. His skin started to glow a little more, but Mercy made no move to stop him, so I assumed that magic was not being used. Apparently, Arturo just glowed when he was intent on killing something.

I reached up and scratched at the still-healing burn on my neck. It was better, but it itched whenever Arturo got close. And, frankly, it only made me more resolved to go through with this plan. The giants may have been the only ones doing incredibly stupid things like kidnapping dragon eggs, dealing in Dragonwort, or setting a bounty on Baz's head, but the exousia were just as volatile, just as dangerous. For all I knew, they were doing things just as stupid as the giants, only far more subtle. The mortal realms might have needed them to keep the balance of magic in place, but I did not have to like them.

Arturo sucked in a sharp breath and then exhaled swiftly, driving his sword straight towards the bear. There was a clang and a sort of *crack* and suddenly I was glad that I stood a few feet away from the statues. The sword broke off a small portion of the concrete right around the bear's heart; this piece of concrete then sailed through the air and shattered on the ground by the table. The sword, though, skittered along the statue's length and wrenched itself out of Arturo's hand.

Tiberius started laughing. Guffawing, really. He bent over and clutched at his stomach, eyes screwed tight and tears of mirth spilling over his face. Not terribly dignified, but not unsurprising, either. Even Mercy could not resist rolling her eyes.

Arturo snarled wordlessly and lunged towards Tiberius, hands shining with that burning power. Mercy coughed once, mildly, and the exousia halted in his tracks, shoulders heaving as he breathed heavily.

"How deep is the break?" Mercy asked in a cold voice, gaze directed unflinchingly at Arturo, who was now steaming. Baz snatched a ruler off the table and put it up to the bear, which looked somehow improved now that it was missing a piece.

"Nine centimetres," Baz said, squinting at the ruler. "And a smidge."

Tiberius laughed harder.

"Sir Giant," Mercy said, and the coldness in her voice was now an ice storm. The giant straightened, wiping tears from his eyes, and grinned. "Take up your weapon. Your statue is in the centre."

Tiberius sketched a bow. "With pleasure, Lady Mercy. I will prove to all of you what strength really is."

Tiberius grabbed his sword, holding it in his fist like it was a club or a cricket bat or something equally un-swordlike. Arturo let out a furious snort, but simply shuffled towards the table with his arms crossed.

Now, I hadn't been terribly worried about the exousia's display of strength. From my encounters with Arturo and his people, they seemed quite skilled but not possessed of that otherworldly strength that some immortals displayed. But Tiberius was a giant. Granted, he was technically only a partial manifestation of a sleeping giant's mind, but he was still strong. I had no idea what the relative breaking point of concrete was, but I rather thought if he were able to kick and punch the statue, it would crumble into oblivion. Hence the sword; it was harder to exert the amount of force needed to impale a statue when your tool was a metal sword not borne up by magic. Not impossible, but there was a reason why people used sledgehammers to break things.

Then again, I had not done particularly well in physics at school. This could turn out badly.

I folded my arms and found myself curling my fingers into fists, the slight pressure of my nails digging into my palms close enough to the sensation of pain that I was forced to concentrate on that. Sometimes, I thought it would be useful to actually feel pain normally. Of course, that would mean my many and varied deaths would be much worse, so the thought never persisted.

Tiberius raised the sword and took two swift steps forward, thrusting the blade into the statue as far as it would go. Only, it didn't go. It shattered. There were a couple of concrete chips that went flying, but none as large as the one Arturo carved away. And the sword itself splintered, metal shearing off into fragments and flying towards us innocent bystanders. Or me, really, since Baz was just behind me.

I ducked and one of the fragments caught in my arm, slicing a long, shallow line into my forearm. I yelped.

Mercy eyed me. "You're fine."

"Thank you for your vote of confidence," I grumbled. "Well, what's the damage?"

Baz wandered over to the statue, circling around the back to avoid getting close to Tiberius, who was gaping at his sword with teeth gritted and shoulders tense. My cousin measured the dent in the statue. "Ten centimetres. Barely."

"What?!" Arturo screeched, the sound almost bird-like. "He injured one of the contenders!"

"Cal's fine," Mercy said. "Right?"

"Yes, fine," I muttered, wiping at the few droplets of blood with my thumb. It stung, like the worst kind of paper cut, and I had to wonder what it would have been doing if my pain receptors were functioning properly. "It was an accident. Probably."

Arturo looked as though he was going to protest, but he shook his head and growled something unpleasant under his breath. Tiberius dropped the broken sword hilt onto the ground, his grimace transformed to a grin.

"I win," he said, jabbing a finger towards Arturo.

"Not yet," Mercy said. "There is still Cal's performance to take into account. As well, we must consider the results of the first challenge. Cal, proceed."

I briefly considered rolling my eyes. Baz nudged me in the shoulder, making me stumble forwards. I sighed and grabbed the sword; it was surprisingly heavy. Still, it was extremely sharp and would do what I needed. I hoped.

I approached the remaining statue and quietly asked Life to try not to interfere with things. I don't think she heard me, or would have complied even if she had, but it made me a little less shaky. I lifted the sword, trying to remember the various stances I had seen in movies and television shows. One elbow lifted, the other close to my body, I swayed backwards and then surged forwards with all the strength in my puny human body.

The sword did exactly what I expected it to do. It halted for a brief moment when I first touched the statue, then slid through like butter. A second later, during which I'm fairly certain I blinked, and the sword was impaled into the styrofoam up to the hilt, a good half of the sword sticking out the other side.

"Right," I said. "That went well."

16

HOUSE AND HOME

As I'm sure you can imagine, that little display did not go over well with Tiberius and Arturo. One fluke win was acceptable; perhaps I had some sort of weird ability that allowed me to be super fast, or teleport or whatever. But two fluke wins? Yeah, that was harder to swallow.

"You used some sort of magic," Arturo said, jabbing a finger at me. As his skin was currently glowing, and I was still healing from the burns he had given me a few days ago, I stepped backwards.

"Nope, no magic." I held up my hands and shrugged. "Scout's honour."

"You were never a scout," Baz said.

"Not helping."

"He was not using magic," Mercy said, voice terse. She was standing behind the table with her hands folded neatly in front of her, as calm as the statues we had just impaled, and far prettier. Arturo glared at her, but did not argue. Tiberius, though, argued.

"You are biased," the giant snapped, taking an imposing step forwards, his foot causing the ground to crack as he moved. Mercy narrowed her eyes.

"I am devoted to the balance," she said, and there was more than a hint of fury in her voice at any suggestion to the contrary. "I do not *have* biases, unless it is *against* Cal."

This confused the giant enough for him to wrinkle his nose. I nodded agreement. "It's true. Mercy does actually hate me. Proven fact and all that."

This statement did not appear to clear up Tiberius' confusion. In fact, it made Arturo wrinkle his nose, too. They looked at each other, remembered the fact that they were competing, and looked away with furious scowls. Baz stepped up and clapped me on the shoulder. I elbowed him in the gut to keep him from saying anything that would make matters worse.

"As it stands," Mercy said, eyes narrowed. "The two competitors are tied. Arturo Siderian has prevailed over Tiberius in the matter of speed. Tiberius has prevailed over Arturo Siderian in the matter of strength. The fact that Cal Thorpe has surpassed both of you in both challenges brings into question your ability to rule *at all*."

Both Arturo and Tiberius started protesting at the top of their lungs, and I'm fairly certain they would have killed me had they been able. Mercy held up a hand and they fell silent, glaring resentfully at me.

"The fact of the matter is that the competition to see who is better suited to rule over the mortal realms did not include Cal in that consideration. He is meant to act as a neutral score, to judge where your abilities lie. As you have been greatly disappointing, I would depose both of you and seek new rulers."

Again, the exousia and giant started protesting, this time adding a good deal of arm flailing to their shouting. Mercy lifted her chin, nostrils flaring, looking absolutely terrifying and magnificent as she stared down these entities. Once more, they both fell into silence. "That provision is not up to me, however. Cal Thorpe is the one who has been given the authority to bestow power. I am merely to judge which is superior. The current matter of the scores, though, means that a restructuring of tomorrow's challenge is in order. The task of intelligence was to start with the lowest score competing against Cal before challenging the higher score. As Cal *is* the higher score, you two will compete directly against each other before moving on."

This statement went over precisely as expected, which was to say, not well. Tiberius and Arturo glared at each other, then glared at me with a good deal more vehemence than I thought the situation warranted. Granted, I had been cheating. They didn't know that. Still, I had the distinct feeling that they now hated me more than they hated one another.

It wasn't an unfamiliar sensation, though, so I ignored it.

"Alright, gentlemen," I said. "Meet here once more

tomorrow morning. We'll sort everything out then. And if neither of you manage to defeat me, then I'll consider Mercy's suggestion that we find new rulers."

After the requisite amount of grumbling, Arturo and Tiberius left, unspoken threats passing between them. Baz, Mercy and I packed up, leaving instructions for the delivery people about the removal of the statues. I didn't know where they were going, but apparently some country estate wanted them for something. Weirdly, the fact that they had been used in "performance art" made them more valuable. It was better than just throwing them away, I suppose. At least the city of London had enough sense to not want them.

Baz and Mercy and I went home for another night of lounging around waiting for things to happen. We tried not to worry over the dragon eggs in Baz's room, and my mother made noises about how annoying it was to have to feed unexpected house guests who couldn't give a definitive date for leaving, though she was unerringly polite about it. I made a note on my phone to send some money after I went back to Elsewhere.

Oddly, I wasn't really missing Elsewhere. I mean, feeling nothing, I wasn't really missing much of anything, but intellectually, I knew that Elsewhere was home now and this place, while containing family, was more of a stopover. I imagined that it would be nice to see Yolanda again, and Agravane— though he was likely to act less than enthused to see me once he realised I wasn't done with taking pictures for the coffee marketing campaign. I even thought about my almost-relationship with Neja, though the djinn wandered about more than I did, and we never had any firm plans to see one another. Even knowing that my friends were in a whole different realm, I found that being in London, with Baz and my mother, and even Mercy, was comfortable.

Yes, there was the imminent threat of world destruction, but frankly, that wasn't new. Yes, Baz had changed, and I had changed, and we weren't entirely sure what to do with one another. Yes, my mother was as undemonstrative as ever. Yes, I couldn't interact with people I used to know without them forgetting me five seconds after they spoke to me. Yes, people wanted to kill me. All of this should have put a damper on things, but really, I found I sort of enjoyed sitting on the couch watching television over a carton of Chinese food. At least, I assume the warm feeling in my chest was enjoyment and not indigestion. With my condition, it was hard to tell.

Somewhere in the middle of the comedy show, I began to think about going back to Elsewhere. It was inevitable. Death had only given me two weeks vacation, after all. I wondered if I would be able to visit, or if my family would forget once more that I existed. Almost instantly, that warm feeling dissipated. I lay up all night on the couch thinking about it, even going so far as to wake Sebastian up and think a question in its direction. True to form, Sebastian just turned over and went back to sleep. That didn't actually improve matters.

When Mercy came to wake me up, I was already showered and dressed, this time wearing one of Baz's few button-up shirts. My mother had pressed it last night, and Baz seemed frankly cheered that it should be going to me, as if he would much rather have his band t-shirts. Mercy, on the other hand, was wearing her usual medieval style dress, the lacings tight all the way up the front, the sleeves long and a sword at her waist.

"You look...dangerous," I said, blurting out the first thing that came to mind. To my surprise, Mercy favoured me with a slight smile.

"Thank you. I find the fashions of the mortal realm quite uncomfortable, but my other dress was spotted with blood and it is such a pain to get out without brownies helping. Your mother found this in a costume shop." Mercy picked at the skirt.

"It's nice," I said absently, but she was already walking away, moving towards the kitchen. My mother was nowhere to be seen, as it was her day off and she usually slept in. Baz was dressed and eating a pastry, looking cheerful.

"Cal!" he said, grinning at me around a mouthful of frosting. "We should go out to dinner or something when all this is done."

"It is not done yet," Mercy said. "I will admit that this plan has gone better than I anticipated, but it is far from over. These are—"

"Powerful beings," Baz interrupted with a roll of his eyes. "Yes, yes, we know. Can't you just have faith in Cal for a moment? He's never let me down, not once."

"Except when I died." I didn't mean for the words to spill out, but I hadn't yet had my coffee. Besides that, they were true. Baz faltered a bit, a shudder passing through his shoulders, and looked down at the table.

"Yeah, except for that."

Mercy looked between me and Baz, and I thought I saw a flicker of pity in her eyes. She opened her mouth to say something, then shook her head and went about making toast. I wanted to reach out to Baz and try to reassure him, try to make him feel less useless, but I didn't know how. Even before losing my soul, such conversations had been incredibly difficult for me. I could sell just about anything, make it shine and dazzle the world of social media, but connecting with people was something more difficult.

Even when those people were family.

Or perhaps *especially* when those people were family.

"I..." I swallowed my words and tried not to choke. "I'll talk to Death when I get back. See if I can't arrange a few more visits."

Baz flashed a weak smile. "That would be nice."

I winced.

No one seemed to have anything to add, so we finished breakfast in silence, then went about ordering a car to take us to the park. I began to think that Mercy had done something to ward people away, because once again, there was no one there to interfere. Just us, the trees, and the achingly pleasant day. A tingle went up my spine that had nothing to do with emotion. I looked around to try and identify it, but nothing jumped out at me, literally or otherwise. That was not a good sign.

This time, the set up was already done for us; at the far end of the park, next to a pleasant fountain with a huge array of shining coins at the bottom, were several stone tables with benches and chess boards set into the tables. The pieces were laid out, ready for use. It was almost sad, seeing the empty tables and knowing what it was that I had to do.

I prepared to do it, anyways. The feeling along my spine intensified, until it was almost an electrical shock. I ignored it.

Not long after seven, the giant and exousia appeared, Tiberius stepping from the shadows of the trees and Arturo simply appearing in a shaft of sunlight. They had none of the swagger of the last two challenges, none of that impossible confidence, none of the assurance that the world was theirs for the taking. They just approached, watching me warily.

"Please, sit." Mercy gestured to one of the tables with a sweep of her hand. Tiberius eyed the sword at her hip and flicked his gaze to Arturo. The exousia pressed his mouth into a thin line.

They sat.

"This last test is a test of intelligence, of strategy and cunning. You are to play chess, Tiberius taking the white pieces and Arturo the black, until such time as one of you has captured the king of the other. Do you understand?" Mercy looked at each of them firmly.

"How do we know that Cal has the authority he claims?" Arturo asked. He curled his hands around the edge of the table and I could have sworn that smoke curled into the air.

"Do you doubt me?" Mercy rested her hand on the hilt of her sword. As a threat, it was hardly worrying; there were two of them and only one of her, and though I might get involved, I wouldn't be able to do much but act as a punching bag.

"You said it yourself," Tiberius growled, resting a fist on the edge of the table. "You are devoted to the balance. In allowing one of us to win, the balance would suffer."

"In allowing your squabble to continue, there would be no point to the balance at all. There would be nothing left." To my surprise, it was Baz who spoke, a hardness in his voice that I had never heard before. He did not look at me, nor at Mercy. He just stared Tiberius down, fists clenched at his sides. The giant held Baz's gaze.

"This is all a little too contrived," Arturo finally said. Baz flinched at the heat in the exousia's words. "I will grant that as an emissary of Death, Cal has the potential to be...changed. So his speed was acceptable. *Or* his strength. But both? To be outclassed so completely, by a human, no matter what abilities

Death has bestowed upon him, it is inconceivable. Impossible, if you will."

I tried to come up with something clever to say that would turn their attention, change the direction of the conversation. As capable as I usually found my mind, there were only empty thoughts left. They were calling my bluff, and I could not answer for it. This whole scheme hinged on them not looking too closely, not asking questions while they were pitted against one another. I was meant to be the trick, the illusion, and they were their own distractions.

Only, I hadn't counted on them actually communicating with one another, as they obviously had been.

Arturo and Tiberius were opposites, working in opposition in order to balance out the inherent instability of magic in the mortal realms. I had assumed that because of this, they wouldn't cooperate. But Life and Death were opposites, and they were *married*.

I had made a mistake, and now everything was going to fall apart. Worse than that, though, was the fact that Baz was standing between them and me.

I saw the moment that the giant and exousia decided to attack. As one, their muscles tensed and I knew that they would have exploded upwards from the table a moment later, shredding through Baz to get to Mercy and myself. I wouldn't be able to do a thing about it.

They stood. Reached.

Before I could do *anything*, Arturo was behind Baz, a knife to my cousin's throat. Tiberius was between me and them, his hands up and curled into fists, ready to defend himself. The problem with opposites was that when they decided to work together, it was bad. Really, really bad.

I made a sound in my throat and slid into the fighting stance that Agravane had tried so hard to drill into my head. It felt right. Natural. My hands came up. Before Tiberius could so much as sneer at me, I flew at him, ready to claw him to pieces. It didn't matter that this was the first time ever that anything Agravane had taught me meant something. It didn't matter that I was running on pure fury and panic, Sebastian awake and bristling inside me. I was facing off against a giant.

Tiberius punched me hard enough to shatter my jaw. I flew sideways, barely managing to stay on my feet. Baz screamed, the sound enough to waken Sebastian fully, and we both turned our attention to Arturo. The exousia's lips were drawn back, revealing sharp teeth, eyes blazing with that terrible fire. As one, Sebastian and I snarled.

I was vaguely aware of some voice in the background, but the words meant nothing to me. I stepped forwards, a cloud of impossible darkness enveloping my hands, my legs, stretching forwards like some terrible mist. It was the same black-hole colour as Death himself, with sparks of everchanging Life flaring in the dark. Around me, the world turned grey and still, with no colour whatsoever but for the yellow auras surrounding each living person. It was like it had been with the chimera, only more. The lack of colour was deeper, the yellow brighter. I was not fighting for myself, defending myself, but Baz.

Tiberius took one step backwards, hands going up again. I saw the yellow-gold aura that surrounded him expanding to the ground beneath his feet, as though a part of him was there. Silver shards wove through his aura. The exousia had the same yellow-gold and silver lifeforce, only his extended upwards, taking the shape of clouds.

I reached forwards, fingers stretching so that I could touch just a part of that lifeforce. Sebastian roared, the sound echoing out through my own throat. I needed no ability to fight now. No need to punch or kick or use a sword to decapitate my enemies. No, I needed only to touch their lifeforce and they would bow before me, their very existence bound to my whim. I touched the yellow aura of Tiberius and Arturo simultaneously and both beings stiffened, their mouths working without sound, their eyes horrified.

Baz pushed away from Arturo, his own pitiful lifeforce pulsating in time with his heart. He darted behind Mercy, and when he looked back with fear and awe and terror in his entire body, it was not to the giant or the exousia, but to *me* that he looked. That look should have been enough to stop me, to put an end to my rage, but I had the lifeforce of both giant and exousia in my grasp. If I took it, if I devoured it, then I would get more than a moment's worth of feeling, as I had with the chimera.

I could feel things for a whole week.

I licked my lips at the thought and Sebastian snarled in agreement. I tightened my grip, the only sign that Tiberius or Arturo felt anything was the tightness of their breath.

Before I could kill them and exact my revenge, as well as getting access to real emotion, pain shattered my spine. I released their lifeforce and tried to suck in a breath to dispel the pain. It remained. Blood gurgled into my throat and I looked down to see the tip of Mercy's knife protruding through my abdomen, dripping with spinal fluid and blood. I had enough wherewithal to look over my shoulder at her, though the whiteness of my encroaching death tinged my vision.

"You are *bound*," Mercy said, voice ringing out over the courtyard as though someone had rung a bell. She bared her teeth at me, digging in the knife and sending bolts of impossible agony through me. Immediately, Sebastian retreated. The dark mist vanished and I once again became myself, whatever that was. Mercy's eyes softened for a moment, and I could have sworn there was pity there. And sorrow.

"Remember why we're here," she murmured, then pulled out her knife. I fell to my knees and died. Whiteness overtook my vision and I was once again in that familiar place where I went between my deaths and my recovery. Sometimes I heard a voice, and sometimes I didn't. This time, I *felt* sadness. It was not my sadness, but the void around me pulsated with it. Then, as with every time this happened, I blinked and was back in my body, completely healed and once more alive.

When I came to some sort of awareness of the world around me, I realised that Baz was kneeling next to me, his hand on my shoulder, expression concerned. Mercy stood in front of me, speaking to Arturo and Tiberius. "You agreed to complete the challenge. To continue balancing the magic of this realm and to not interfere with the other competitors or their families until such time as the challenge was completed. You are sworn, and you will uphold your bargain or I will enact a blood curse on you and yours for being forsworn."

I had no idea what a blood curse was, or what the general reaction would be to breaking a vow, but the highly powerful entities intent on killing seemed to understand exactly. As one, they sank back into their seats and stared at each other. Arturo grew pale. Tiberius could have had smoke coming from his ears.

"We will play," Tiberius announced, eyes flashing at me. "And when we are done, you will bear the consequences for your insolence and arrogance. Did you think you could threaten our lives with no repercussions? There are *rules*, Emissary of Death."

I nodded. What else could I do?

Mercy held out her hands over the board. "As previously stated, the champion shall be the one who captures their opponent's king."

Tiberius and Arturo sat again, glaring at each other.

"Are you alright, Cal?" Baz asked.

"I'm fine," I said, and it was true. "Though I can't say the same for your shirt." There was a gaping bloody hole in the front of my borrowed shirt, though the skin beneath was unblemished.

"It's okay," Baz said. He helped me to my feet. "Thanks for defending me, even if you were terrifying."

"It was the right thing to do. And you're family. I'll always defend you."

The smile that Baz gave me was genuine, and probably more than I deserved. I would have discussed it with him, but we had a chess game to oversee and the fate of the mortal realms to sort out.

I approached the board from the other side. Mercy looked at me once, and for once, the question in her eyes was perfectly clear. Was I certain about this? I blinked once in acknowledgement. She nodded and folded her hands behind her back.

"One moment gentlemen," I said, reaching out to the pieces. "I need to adjust something."

I put my hands on their kings and snatched the pieces away, just as Mercy spoke the final word, "Begin!"

I expected destruction. I expected fire and brimstone and righteous fury that would shred my flesh from my bones. I expected, especially after that confrontation, that I would be immediately crippled for breaking the vow I had made not to interfere with the competitors. None of this happened. Instead, the giant and exousia turned to stone, eyes trapped somewhere between horror and wrath. Without their kings, they could not complete their challenge, and would forever be locked in a game of chess.

It was a cruel fate. I did not need access to my emotions to know this. I could not die, by whatever mistake of the universe, so being trapped for eternity was literally my worst nightmare. Yet I had just trapped Tiberius and Arturo in that very nightmare, forever. None of their people could come after me, since the game was ongoing. The balance of the mortal realm was protected.

I had won.

It did not seem like much of a victory.

"Thank you," I said to Mercy, voice low. "You stopped me. I don't know what would have happened if you hadn't stopped me. I know that trapping them wasn't the honourable thing, or even the merciful thing, but...it is better than what I would have done to them."

Mercy sighed and scrubbed a hand over her features. I was fairly certain my glasses must have been really smudged, because it almost looked like she was wiping away tears. "Cal, they were not wrong. I am devoted to the balance, for that is the most merciful way of the world. Not for everyone. But for the majority, it is. It hurts now, more than you could ever conceive, but it was the only way."

I reached out to touch Mercy on the arm—for what purpose, I don't know—but she jerked away. "I will not forget this, Cal," she said. "The needs of the many may well outweigh the needs of the few, but that doesn't make it any less painful. And you, for all your clever words and new ways of thinking, caused that pain. Killing you righted no wrongs, only brought about more pain."

"Even after all that, you still hate Cal? After all he did to help the balance?" Baz demanded. He stood at my side, arms folded, expression indignant. Mercy looked at him, expression flat, empty. Then, she walked away.

"Hey, wait!" Baz called after her. I grabbed his wrist and shook my head.

"Leave her be, Baz," I said. "Her part in this is done. I have caused her enough suffering without trying to change her mind."

"But you didn't do anything wrong!"

I sighed and stared at the stone figures. They looked like art, far more impressive than the pathetic bear statues from the day before. You couldn't see the fire in Arturo's eyes, nor the blue colour of Tiberius' skin. They just looked like two men playing chess. No one would know the fate of the world depended on them.

"Didn't I?" I asked. The weight of the chess pieces in my pocket seemed insurmountable. Part of me wanted to replace them on the board, to let this play out as perhaps it should have done. Part of me wanted to walk away, to leave all of this behind and never look back. If only it were that simple.

"Let's go home," I murmured.

"Maybe we can stop at a coffee shop on the way home?" Baz waggled his eyebrows hopefully. I almost smiled, the thought of coffee filling my mind and making things a little less terrible, even if it didn't last.

We walked back across the park and took a bus home, Baz already launching into a discussion of what his next career should be. He didn't once mention the incident where I had nearly placed the entire mortal realms in jeopardy, and I was grateful for that. We were almost at the house, and I pulled out my phone to text Yolanda the news.

Then, reality fractured. A million tiny pieces of the world fell away. The trees to our right just shivered and were no more, a keening in my mind the only indication they had ever been. I fell to my knees, hands pressed over my ears. Baz was on the ground beside me, mouth working and no discernible sound coming out.

Thud.

I sucked in a desperate breath, my lungs suddenly too small.

Thud.

Sebastian roared to life deep inside me. It surged into my mind, taking possession of my body and raging defiance at the being that stood before me.

Thud.

The dragon took one look at me, bared its fangs in a terrible smile, and laughed.

17

DEFENDING THE HOME

Somehow, though I'm not sure how, I managed to drag my way forwards a few inches and practically threw myself over the still-prone Baz. My cousin was making pitiful screeching noises now, like a bird fallen out of its nest and in the sight of a falcon. He stared unseeing, his hands clawing at his ears. I lay over Baz, keeping him from moving—and probably crushing him in the process, but my heroic efforts are rarely highly effective—and let Sebastian snarl up at the dragon in pure defiance.

My vision changed as it had done when I faced Arturo and Tiberius, as if the terrible power I held could stand a chance against what I now faced. The impossible power of the giant and the starfire of the exousia were *nothing* compared to the dragon and I realised just how stupid I was. How arrogant to think that I could do anything to stop this, to change anything.

Beneath me, Baz glowed a vibrant yellow, pulsing with life wrapped in the throes of abject panic. The cars and paving and houses were all dull and grey, lifeless. My hand, at the corner of my sight, was empty, though not quite as grey as the houses. The dragon, standing before me in a blur of scales and claws and fangs and wings, impossible to mistake and equally impossible to understand fully, was streaked with silver. Immortal. Out of my power. Or it would have been, had not there been a very slight tinge of sickly yellow to its scales.

I reached out to touch, to separate life from being and protect my family. A part of me knew that I could have easily explained the situation, told the dragon everything about finding its eggs, about keeping them from the giants, about imprisoning Tiberius and Arturo to maintain the balance, and all would have been well. This being was obviously intelligent. I had been around wyverns before, and even a strange cat-headed creature called the Tatzelwurm who had a bizarre, one-dimensional view of a convoluted world. Those beings were capable, of course, but they could not compare to the sheer undeniable mental acuity I saw in those great eyes, each as big as my torso. The part of me that knew this, though, was buried beneath the myriad coils of Sebastian.

So I reached for that yellow light, the life of the dragon, prepared to rip it from the creature's bones. It roared in fury, the earth shaking with the force of that sound. A pipe burst through the street not one metre from me. Car alarms went off and then went strangely silent. The world fell away and I knew that this thing was going to kill me over and over and over again for the sheer insolence of trying to stand up to its might. I bared my teeth in defiance and prepared for it, just as ready to defend my family.

A leg, clad in impeccably tailored trousers in a light green wool, with a gleaming red Oxford shoe straight out of a period drama of the World War II years, stepped between the dragon and my reaching hand. It was surrounded by a slightly-faded mortal yellow aura. Strong and confident and absolutely sure of obedience. Sebastian hissed and pulled back, partly in shock and partly in fear. I had never known Sebastian to be afraid before.

The dragon pulled back, too.

I looked up and saw my mother, as straight backed and perfectly coiffed as ever, standing between us. Her expression was flat, though I caught a glimpse of a furrowed brow as I lay on the street on top of Baz. In her arms was a crate that I knew weighed almost fifty pounds. It contained the eggs.

"Kindly step away from my son and nephew," my mother said, voice perfectly calm.

"Thief," the dragon snarled, maw opening with a snap. "Those do not belong to you. Do you know the penalty for stealing the eggs of a being such as I?"

"How could I? Dragons have been absent from this

land for centuries, for a very good reason if I under-stand things correctly." Ah, yes, my mother. Ever logical and absolute. Frankly, I had no idea how she could even stand, let alone form coherent sentences. Beneath me, Baz was still whimpering. Even I felt the pressure of the dragon's presence, though Sebastian was keeping most of that back.

"Insolent human. I will tear you to shreds and then flay your offspring as an example of *why* we are so feared." Even as it spoke, the dragon raised a single talon, ready to strike my mother down. She did not flinch. I did not even think she was impressed.

"I was told your kind were intelligent, powerful, a cut above the rest of the common horde. Yet you resort to petty violence, just as everyone else might. How disappointing."

The dragon hissed, sounding a little like a cat. "Put the eggs down and I will promise to make your death swift."

"Only if you promise not to harm my son, or my nephew," my mother said, making no move to put down the eggs or move away from Baz and myself. Sebastian made a confused sound, and I couldn't tell if it actually came from me, or if I just heard it in my head. Either way, I had no answer.

"And which is your offspring? The simpering fool who cannot stand up to my presence, or the one who will assuredly die slowly for trying to do me harm?" The dragon snaked its head around, peering at Baz and I. My mother gave a polite cough.

"I don't see how that is any of your business. Now, shall we back away from each other slowly, or would you prefer I drop the eggs?" If it were anyone but my mother, I would have questioned whether there was sarcasm involved. She was perfectly serious, though, and apparently even the dragon could sense it. The being curled its lips back, revealing fangs the size of my legs. Baz whimpered, crying like a five-year-old.

"I see your world must be reeducated about proper respect. I will endeavour to teach them once you are gone."

My mother sighed and shook the box gently. "You are certainly very chatty, given the circumstances. Now, please, step back and I shall do the same."

Finally, because it was completely pointless trying to argue with her, the dragon ducked its head in what I assume was a nod. Then, it winked out of existence and reappeared at the end of the street, shattering pavement as it did so. My mother nodded graciously and lowered the box to the ground. She turned to help Baz up and gave me a pointed look. Were I not legally old enough to make my own decisions, I had no doubt I would be grounded. Forever.

Baz was safely standing, though still crying, and I was just about to walk away as well, my eyes on the dragon to make certain there was no treachery involved, when a lorry turned onto the street, speeding along without any care to what might be in the way. My mother and Baz had reached the steps of the house, but I was still in the road, the dragon was at the end of the street, and the box of eggs was about to be run over by a careless driver.

Three things happened simultaneously.

One, the dragon *screamed*. It was not infused with any particular magic, or the world would have fallen apart and I could not have done anything about it. No, this was a scream of terror and horror and inevitability.

Two, the lorry driver saw the dragon and screamed also. Instead of slamming on the brakes, though, the driver accelerated, the engine whining in protest and growing ever closer to the box of eggs. Mercy had said the eggs were likely tough, not needing to be incubated or anything, but they were still eggs and therefore fragile.

Three, I did something that was likely considered incredibly stupid: I leaped onto the eggs, Sebastian curling around me to use whatever protective power it had to keep the yellow-and-silver light emanating from the box intact and alive. I was not quite big enough to cover the entire box, but I could get very, very close.

The lorry slammed into me at the same moment that dragon fire streamed from the beast's maw to disintegrate the lorry and driver. Whatever Reaper power I had remaining flared to life, creating a barrier between the fire and the lorry, instead directing the bulk of the flame towards myself.

If you've ever burned your hand on an oven, you know that a burn starts out hot, but quickly becomes sharp and cold. This was like that, only increased by an exponential degree. My body felt like it had been dumped into the deepest, darkest part of the ocean. My bones popped with the pressure and my flesh melted away. On the other side of me, I was crushed into dust as I lay between the many-tonne lorry and the box of eggs.

It hurt. A lot.

Sadly, I've also had worse.

Familiar white light filled my vision, drawing me into the void and keeping me there for a few beats. It wasn't long enough to know or understand what was on the "other side", if that was indeed what I experienced in these moments when I died, before I came back. This time, I stayed there a little longer, and the voice that I sometimes heard in this empty place gave a sigh.

Back again, are we? And so soon...

It was a familiar voice, but not one I could identify. I sucked in a breath and prepared to respond, but the moment passed and I was suddenly exactly where I had been, the pain little more than a passing soreness.

The lorry was still there, a little singed, but in one piece. The driver had already thrown open the door and was fleeing down the street, wailing at the top of her lungs. I groaned and rolled onto my back, slightly surprised to find that I was hyperventilating. I blinked a couple of times, realising that the blurriness I saw was a product of my glasses having melted into a slag of metal and glass, barely holding shape. I pulled them off my nose and looked around.

I don't know what I expected, but a hand wearing a

leather glove, attached to a suit-clad wrist with expensive cufflinks, holding out a pair of my own glasses, was not it. I took the glasses and slipped them back onto my nose. The dark blur attached to the hand and sleeve resolved itself into Death, looking down at me with a gentle smile.

"Hello," I said with as much politeness as I could muster. "Yolanda managed to get a hold of you."

Death smiled and held out his hand to help me sit up. I took it, only to have a cold breeze travel over my skin. I looked down and yelped. All that was left of my clothing were two chess pieces, laying on the ground. Death lay a blanket over me, hiding me from onlookers. "Dragon fire is terrible on the wardrobe," he said.

I nodded, thankful that I hadn't been wearing my own clothes. "I'll have to buy Baz a new shirt. And trousers. And shoes."

"Oh, for crying out loud!" Life's voice broke into my musings and I turned to find her standing a few feet away, as terrible and wonderful as ever, scowling. She folded her arms. "You can't even do death scenes properly!"

"I think the death part was fine," Death said. "It's the coming back to life bit that was perhaps unconventional."

His wife huffed and tossed her head. "Very well. What person comes back and starts making shopping lists?!"

"To be fair," I said, standing and wrapping the

blanket around me, "I have come back before. I can't go being dramatic *every* time."

Life glared at me.

I think it was probably her presence that knocked me back into my own, because I finally took the time to look around and assess the situation. The dragon was crooning over the eggs, which were apparently unharmed. It looked remarkably less fearsome when making doe-eyes at the colourful eggs. Baz was sitting on the steps to the house, mouth open and eyes wide as he stared at the dragon and Life and Death. My mother was standing just a little in front of him, hands on her hips, looking more annoyed than I had seen her since that time Baz used dish soap in the washing machine.

"Perhaps, Cal, we could go inside and have a cup of tea—or coffee, if you would prefer—so that no more innocent bystanders come to harm?" Death asked, ever reasonable. I nodded and shrugged, picking my way along the street and trying not to step on anything uncomfortable or unidentifiable.

Just as I passed the dragon, it lifted its head. The eyes were still wary, still barely containing the fury within. But it gave a gracious nod, which I think was meant for Death, then wrapped a massive talon around the box and vanished from sight. I felt a little tremor in the world, nothing like when it had first arrived, and knew it was gone.

So much for gratitude.

Not to mention, the street was still torn to bits.

As I passed my mother on the way into the house, I said, "Perhaps you should consider moving to the country, in case I visit again."

She nodded. "I was just thinking that."

We went inside.

18

GOING HOME

It turns out that Baz didn't have any more clean clothes that looked anything like what a respectable business person might wear. So I ended up coming back down to the kitchen in a pair of jeans and Baz's Tiny Dinosaurs With Phasers shirt. My mother, in the middle of making a pot of coffee, took one look at me and snorted a laugh.

"Not helping," I grumbled.

"It suits you. For a casual weekend sort of thing. I suppose."

Baz, on the other hand, grinned fiercely, apparently completely recovered from his earlier trauma. "Hey, that fits you better than it does me!" He pulled out his phone and snapped a picture. I scowled at him.

Life and Death had not gone, as a quiet part of me hoped they would. Instead, they were seated at opposite sides of the tiny table. Death already had a cup of tea in a saucer, and Life was stress-eating a plate of biscuits. Baz started wandering towards her, a dazed look in his eye. I shot my hand out and grabbed his wrist.

"Trust me," I said. "It's better if you stand on the other side of the kitchen."

"But Aunt Teresa gets to sit at the table!" Baz protested.

"That is because I am not a fool," my mother said evenly. Baz sighed dramatically, but did as he was asked, grumbling all the while. I clapped him on the shoulder and sat next between Life and Death. My mother poured two cups of coffee, handed one to me, then sat in the vacant chair.

"So," she said, sipping at the liquid. She wrinkled her nose. "I don't understand how you can drink this at all hours, Cal."

"Practise," I said.

Death chuckled. "You are certainly a singular family," he said. My mother stared blankly at him. I did the same, though I'm sure not for the same reasons.

"You're the one who took my son away," she said, expression flat. Life snickered, which drew my mother's attention. "And you're the one who has caused him all sorts of difficulty."

Life shrank into her chair and I think I might have fainted with shock had I not been busy enjoying the euphoria of coffee. Sebastian blinked with alarm.

"Cal has been far more of an asset than I could have anticipated," Death said, his voice poised to charm and soothe. It must have worked, because my mother relaxed her shoulders ever so slightly. "You must be proud."

"Indeed," my mother replied, which was about the most praise I had ever heard her give. "Cal always did have a certain flair for fixing things other people broke. It's his own problems he is hopeless at handling."

Life opened her mouth to make a retort, but Death held up his hand. They glared at each other for a moment before Life stuck her tongue out at her husband and stuffed another biscuit into her mouth.

"As I said, a valuable asset," Death said. He looked at me, at my mother, at Baz, then sighed. "You know I cannot prevent what is about to happen, correct?"

"You're going to take Cal away again. Even after all he did to save me," Baz whispered. I was struck by the amount of devastation in his voice, and I turned to look at him. He swiped a hand at his eyes. "It's not fair."

"Life isn't fair," Life sneered. The table jerked and Death sank a swift kick into my leg.

"Ow!" I yelped.

"Ah, sorry," Death murmured. "My aim was off."

Life smirked and I had the sudden urge to kick her as well. Baz gave a loud sniffle.

"I am sorry," Death said, looking between the two. "But Cal has been removed from the fate of the world. He cannot stay in the mortal realms for long periods of time. Things would...unravel."

"It seems that he is fairly well connected to the fate

of the world, considering you sent him here to sort out the balance of the mortal realms." Once again, the delivery was emotionless—or nearabouts, for anyone who did not know her—but I could tell. My mother was *furious*.

"Hey, Mum," I said, reaching out to take her hand. She turned to me and her eyes softened slightly. "It's okay."

"I simply wish to make the circumstances clear," she replied. "Drink your coffee."

"Yes, Mum," I said, dutifully taking a sip. Death watched this in silence, a contemplative expression crossing his features. Life just rolled her eyes, eloquent as ever.

"May I ask, Mrs. Thorpe," Death said, "what you felt when, ah, speaking with the dragon?"

"I don't see what business that is of yours."

"I merely wish to know whether you felt the dragon's presence in your mind. It usually has a dramatic effect on...humans."

Baz gave an uncomfortable shrug and looked down at his drink. I saw a faint tinge of red on his tan cheeks. I'd tell him he didn't have to be embarrassed, but bringing it up in front of company would only make things worse. I'd tell him later. In fact, I'd even have a whole conversation with him about how there was no shame in being human, about needing protection from the immortal beasties out there. If Death and Life allowed it, that is.

My grip tightened on the coffee mug, and for once, the scent did not tantalise me as it usually did.

My mother shrugged one shoulder with the sort of casual elegance it takes a lifetime to practise. "It was mildly uncomfortable," she said. "Like listening to the neighbours yell over a football match. Little more."

Life propped her elbows on the table and gave a maliciously intrigued grin. "How *interesting*."

My mother ducked her chin at Life, then pointedly raised her brows. "Ahem."

To my utter astonishment, Life blushed and took her elbows off the table. Death leaned back in his chair, looking as though he was moments away from gaping. "Interesting indeed," he said. "I did not know any of your kind still existed. It does explain a lot about Cal, however."

"Oh, you can't be serious," Life said. "*Her*? A Knight?"

"I have not been given that particular honour," my mother said with a touch of ice in her voice, as if the thought of the queen bestowing a knighthood upon her was a little beyond the realm of reason. It seemed a little improbable, given that we were having tea with Life and Death and had just dealt with a dragon trying to destroy the street, but such was my mother.

"Ah, yes, not the knight as you know it, that title granted by your human royalty. No, the mantle of Knighthood harkens back to a time when dragons actually roamed the mortal realms freely. They were the ones who ultimately were responsible for slaying a good number of dragons, and the reason for their eventual departure. They were humans of particular mettle, though it has been suggested there is magic somewhere in their bloodline. A hereditary calling." Death nodded solemnly. He gave a wistful sort of sigh. "I had thought they died out centuries ago. It does explain why Cal so readily adapted to his role as a Reaper."

"I won't be working for you," my mother said evenly. She fixed a firm glance at Life. "Or you."

Life rolled her eyes again. "Oh, yes, definitely a Knight. So sanctimonious!"

"Hey!" Baz and I protested, each of us straightening our backs in indignation. Death chuckled. My mother simply sipped at her coffee.

"In any case, good lady," Death said. "I must bring Cal back with me. He will be allowed to visit, and communicate by telephone or that ridiculous social media if you like, but he cannot stay."

"Once a year at the holidays," my mother said simply. "And no excuses."

Death blinked and looked a little taken aback. He glanced at me and I shrugged. As if *I* could do anything about her. Then, "Very well. Cal, we must be getting on."

Sebastian and I exchanged a glance. I set the coffee mug on the table. "Shouldn't we perhaps discuss the situation with the giants and exousia?"

"I don't see *why*," Life complained, already rising. She'd eaten all the biscuits. "They're contained. You fixed the balance. Bully for you and all that nonsense."

"My dear." Death gave an exasperated sigh. "What, in particular, did you want to discuss?"

"I nearly stole their lifeforce for attacking Baz. Mercy had to kill me to make me stop. Then, I tricked them," I said. Mercy's disappointed look flashed in my mind and it took more effort than I expected to push it away. "I used a loophole in a sworn oath to trick them into an eternity of...I don't know what you'd call it."

"And yet, the mortal realms are stable," Death said. "You have not had proper training in your Reaper abilities, so it is no wonder it took physical harm to halt your attack. There is a reason there are no more Reapers. What you did to enforce stability, as I understand it, was not breaking a vow, but, as you said, using a loophole. It was not wrong. Though, word of it will get around and such things will not be so simple in the future. It was, however, effective. "

"Not wrong?" Baz let out a dark laugh. "Cal is the best guy I know, and he had to cheat to win at some stupid competition because you lot couldn't sort out how to maintain the balance of the mortal realms properly."

"It is not in *our* jurisdiction," Life said with a pretty —and cruel—smile. Baz flushed from head to toe, but he stood his ground and stared her down.

"Then why did Cal need to get involved?" he

snapped. Life blinked and tilted her head, tapping her chin with her finger.

"What a good question," she said, and promptly vanished. I could have sworn I heard her laughing in the void she left behind. Death sighed and stood.

"It was necessary," Death said softly. "The reason why would shatter your mortal mind, but it was truly necessary." He looked at Baz and smiled, though not nearly so sharply as Life. "Your loyalty to Cal is commendable, but this is the way the world works. In order to do what is necessary, sometimes the rules must be broken. Bent. Loopholes created."

Baz narrowed his eyes, then he did the bravest thing I've ever seen him do. He stepped forward and stood toe to toe with Death. Raised his chin. Puffed out his chest. And said, with all the finality of belief, "No."

Death smiled, this time with enough sharpness to match Life. "Well, well, a remarkable family indeed. I think I might have a job for you, Basil Thorpe. There is a role that has not been filled for some time, and voids are ever so bothersome."

"What role?" Baz asked, sounding suspicious.

"Justice."

I nearly choked on my coffee.

Baz opened his mouth to ask questions, but Death held up a hand. "I'll be in touch. Mrs. Thorpe, thank you for the tea. I'll promise to have Cal home in time for the holidays. Ta ta!"

Death grabbed my arm, and before I could so much as protest, transported me back to Elsewhere.

The last thing I heard was Baz muttering, "Justice? What in the world does *that* mean?"

I had a feeling things were about to get a whole lot more complicated. And I hadn't even finished my coffee.

he End.

ACKNOWLEDGMENTS

As always, these books may spring from my brain, but they could not exist without support. Namely, from *your* support, dear reader. But there are some specific people I'd like to thank for this book.

My cover designer, Fay Lane, who is, without a doubt, a genius. Her work is always fantastic, and I love seeing what she comes up with for these books (and a bunch of others, too). They embody the snark of this series perfectly, and give it a bit of class, too.

Then my publicist/editor, Michael Evan, who doesn't bat an eye at the strange scenarios that take place within these pages. Partly because his books are also weird and awesome, but that's a different story entirely. (One worth reading.)

And, of course, my family, who no longer thinks that the things coming out of my head are beyond the realm of the believable; they're just the realm of fiction.

Thank you. All.

ABOUT THE AUTHOR

E.G. Stone is an independent author who has been writing, creating and causing vast amounts of trouble since the age of six. Since then, E.G. has improved rather a lot in both the trouble-causing and writing and now spends her time writing fantasy and science fiction. When not writing, she is off musing about the workings of languages, both real and created, or drawing and sewing. E.G. reads voraciously, perhaps to the point of slight-insanity. Weird, nerdy, perhaps a little crazy, she is having a grand old time writing, reading, reviewing, interviewing, and, naturally, continuing her endeavours in causing trouble.